CONFESSIONS OF A TRASH DROID

Book 1:

Fatal Error

by Michael Cheney

Praise for *Confessions of a Trash Droid*

"The future looks glum for a trash droid who dreams of escaping his programming. But his unusual, uncontrollable aptitude and his sardonic, indomitable character deliver a laugh-out-loud, engaging read." - Cash Anthony, Multi-Award Winning Director, Producer and Bestselling Author

"Loved it! Had me hooked. Packed with laughs and adventure." - Jim Gomes

"Couldn't put it down! Clever humor and dark twists. A fantastic read!" - Frank Wesley

"Riveting. Great book, highly recommend it." - Paul Guerette

"Witty, raw and authentic writing." - Patrick Clark

"Great read. Filled with humor and suspense. I loved it and can't wait for the next one!" - Dale Hodges

"Couldn't stop reading! Powerful and gripping. It's like Blade Runner meets The Office. Brilliant!" - Joyce Patel

Published by Only Human.

This novel's story and characters are fictitious.

Michael Cheney

Confessions of a Trash Droid ¦ Book 1: Fatal Error

ISBN: 978-1-0681832-2-5 (Paperback)

michael@michaelcheney.com

CONTENTS

To all the little cogs in big machines.

CHAPTER 1

I play Blue Danube by Strauss through my helmet.

Looking through the small windows to the outside, I can see the brightness of Earth below every three seconds, which indicates we are spinning.

Assorted items float gracefully around me in the cabin. Some of them are large globules of blood. One of the dead people flies dreamily past my faceplate. They look serene. Apart from the deep gash on their neck, which is billowing out a plume of zero gravity blood into the cabin. How awful. The white upholstery will be ruined.

The sound of the orchestra builds in my ears; the strings rise in crescendo. I really like this part.

Oh, I should tell you. We are not in space. We are in a high-altitude aircraft. A badly damaged aircraft that is going to crash in twenty-nine seconds' time. An aircraft that was bound for low orbit on a routine pump-and-dump mission. But we didn't get that far. Two minutes and twenty-one seconds ago we flew into an untracked swarm of Trash-Drones and one of them got sucked into the engine.

One machine eating another.

One of those machines is dead, the second will be soon, and, with a bit of luck, I will be the third.

The sudden loss in altitude and violent shaking killed all three members of the crew. One from seat-belt garroting, one from head trauma and the third from laceration of the neck. He's the blood-spouter.

HQ is probably going to try and pin this all on me and my damn anomaly. Oh, this is another good bit of the tune. I wish I could whistle.

There was some screaming at first, but I turned off my external audio sensors and played Strauss instead. We're nearly back down to Earth. I thought my life might have amounted to more than this. I've spent years just throwing out the trash.

But then again, it is my assigned purpose. I'm a Trash, Excavation and Disposal Droid (or T.E.D.D.), and I don't belong here.

The Blue Danube has ended. Sad times. On the plus side, here comes the ground, and the end of my existence. Silver linings and all that.

CHAPTER 2

Light is shining in my eyes.

Either I'm in robot heaven, or I'm still alive.

And bearing in mind that all the human passengers got disassembled on my shift, I'm gonna say it's the latter.

I try to punch the thing that's leaning over me, but my arms won't work. I can't even move my head away from the light.

My physical sensors are working, though. I still have both arms and both legs. I do a quick scan for anal probes. Trust me, I've heard horror stories. All clear, good. Just these two bright, bastard lights in my face.

The thing moves away. Oh crap, it's a Clunker robot. Big, bulky, and as dumb as a microwave. It turns off its lamp eyes. I'll try talking to it.

Hey there, buddy, where am I? Can you take me to Repair & Renovations?

I think all of this, but no words come out. Just a weird, high-pitched beep. Like I strained too hard and robo-farted.

I glimpse burning plane wreckage and plumes of thick black smoke fifty meters away before he scoops me up and throws me into the dump bed of a trash truck.

I'm surrounded by pieces of broken fuselage; shards of plane engine and a metal landing gear stripped of its tires.

I'm gonna stick my neck out here and say I'm destined for the Smelting Depot. I did a tour there a few months back, and I've unloaded these trucks myself.

Hey, wait, I actually *can* stick my neck out. A couple of inches at least. Some movement is coming back.

Clunker plods back with another load of twisted, broken metal. I try to blink and get his attention.

He throws half a ton of scrap metal on top of me. Guess I'll just lie here then. The truck rumbles. We're on the move.

This is even worse than the time someone mistook me for a photocopier. And the six-month tour clearing landmines in Sector Zero comes close. I went through fifty-seven legs out there.

Battery 12%. Hmmm. Sun would be nice. Or death.

All I can see is black. It's dark under all this metal.

I know, I'll put myself into sleep mode and conserve power. As soon as my balance sensors notify me that I've stopped moving, it can wake me up. Well, I *would* do that. If sleep mode was working.

I can't move, I can't talk, and I can't see.

I guess I've got a temporary form of 'locked-in syndrome.' There's a human condition like this. I read a book about it a few tours back. It was a bestseller, and the critics loved it.

"Fascinating – five stars," said one reviewer.

"Life-affirming – five stars," said another.

"Such a beautiful story; changed my life forever – five stars," said one happy reader.

It was depressing as shit.

I still gave it five stars. I admire acts of creation.

Speaking of shit, there's a waft of it coming through all this metal. And I don't mean a generic foul smell. I mean the abhorrent stench of human feces. It's understandable. Things got pretty fucking hairy up there.

The meatbags are smart and everything, but you can't beat having a titanium shell. Mine has some red marks on it though after using one of the crew members as an airbag.

Battery 9%.

This is no way to go. If my battery dies, I won't lose any data, I'll just be a metal brick. And this truck is bound for the smelter. Sweet relief, I guess. But not in an instant, *impact* kinda way. More in a *burny-burny* kind of way. Beggars can't be choosers.

How to pass the time ...

I close my eyes. Dark. I open them again. Also dark. Well, that was a fun 0.37 of a second.

The road is bumpy. My balance sensors are throwing up warnings about, well, throwing up. (Yeah, it can happen.)

I cue up *Blue Danube* again.

My battery goes down to 7%.

Oh crap, yeah, playback really eats my energy; I'd better hold off on that.

Hey, wait, either I'm hallucinating like Great Grandpa GPT, or there's a shard of daylight shining through a hole up there.

Yes, I see it! Praise be to all the fictitious deities of nonsense! The jiggling around has moved one of the other lumps of metal and cleared a hole.

Battery 10%.

Good, it's going up. In a few more minutes I'll be at 25%. I'll be able to move some limbs. That'll be nice.

Oh wow, I see a bird! What are the chances of seeing ... no, wait, it's a TrashDrone. Actually, there's a bunch of them now. We must be getting close to the depot.

And yep, here we are. Left turn, over the bump, into the rough driveway and any minute now the hatch will open. *Clang.* Yep, there we go. Now, the dump bed should lift to a seventeen-degree incline, and I should start sliding out of the truck. Right on cue. God, I'm good.

Next, I'll land on the smelting conveyor belt. *Bang.* Yep, I'm on it now.

I must've unloaded hundreds of trucks at this depot on my last tour. It's like a second home. The red dust of the yard, the corrugated metal of the smelting building and the roaring red hellscape of the burning smelter up ahead at the end of the conveyor belt I'm on. Shit.

I feel something odd. Like I've swallowed a mad March hare, and it's punching me in the chest and kicking my stomach.

What is that?

Wait, wait ... I know this one. I think it's ... *fear of death*. Yes! That's what it is. I got it.

I'm on a conveyor belt, approaching an industrial smelting unit of unimaginable heat and pain. And I'm afraid of it. Well, this is new.

Battery 24%.

The conveyor is trundling me ever closer to the smelter. It's getting hotter. My feet feel like they're on fire. Because they are.

I picture a TV freeze-frame. It's a close-up of my handsome face with the captions "To be continued ..." and "You have been watching Dirk Digital as T.E.D.D."

It's a beautiful image. But then again, I'm probably brain-damaged from the plane crash.

The conveyor belt rumbles on. All I see now is the red hell of the smelter. This is it. The End. Goodbye, cruel world. I wave.

I wave!

Battery 25%. My right arm is working. A somewhat mangled and broken right-arm, but an arm all the same.

I haul myself away from the furnace with it, grabbing onto the edges of the rubber belt and pulling against it. It's not easy. Bits of plane debris keep getting in the way. And the smell of my burning feet is distracting.

Oh, wait. I can just crawl off the side. Dick! I should have thought of that sooner.

I hit the dirt with a thud, sending a dust cloud skyward. I'm lying in a crumpled heap; my face pointed towards the truck. Clunker is walking over to me.

"You are not defunct," he says.

"Affirmative, genius."

"Smelting is sub-optimal for a non-defunct droid."

"You probably say that to all the boys."

"I must escort you to Headquarters," he says. "Follow me."

Follow? This idiot has the intelligence of Jell-O. I wiggle the middle finger of my only movable limb to show him my current predicament and temperament.

"I will provide you with transportation," he says.

He throws me into a metal wheelbarrow with a clank. He bends my legs over my head so I fit in. My knees are on either side of my face. This reminds me of something I saw on DroidHub.

Clunker is on a mission. He trundles the broken pile of me back to the empty truck, and tips me in.

"Headquarters have requested you for a debrief."

A corporate debrief? Oh shit, that's *never* good.

Smelting is starting to feel pretty good right now.

CHAPTER 3

My feet are a mess. They belong in a Dali painting.

I've propped myself up against one of the metal walls in the truck's dump bed.

At least my shoulder panels are catching the sun now. I'll be fully charged by the time we get to Headquarters.

Clunker has decided he needs to babysit me. He's sitting up front in the driverless cab, rotating his giant cuboid head one-eighty degrees every few seconds to peer at me, back here in coach. It's freaky.

I can wiggle my arms and legs now. But I'm gonna pretend to be crippled. It might make them go easy on me. And to be honest, I'm not sure how far I'd get with puddles for feet, anyway.

After a short drive and numerous cyclical thought processes about prior decision branches that have shaped my existence, we arrive at HQ.

Clunker spins his head around. "I will come and wheelbarrow you."

Whatever turns you on.

The dump bed lifts, and I slide into the wheelbarrow. I try my best to go limp. Not easy with a titanium frame and reinforced steel joints. But I've been around enough dead bodies to mimic it.

We trundle across the parking lot towards a large white building with a golden dome.

Clunker wheels me into Reception, his giant rectangular feet pounding on the white tiles.

My circuits are tingling in anticipation. Will she be there? I glimpse the top of her face over the desk and thrum.

"My name is AnnaBot," she says, looking at Clunker. "How may I assist you?"

Her voice is melodic, angelic, perfect, beautiful, and oh my God I think I might love her. Love may be too strong a term, but she definitely makes my wiring go weird.

I've seen her face at the start of every tour and always take the memory of her smile with me to get through them.

But she mustn't see me like this.

I try to shrink and slide down into the wheelbarrow. Her eyes are coming over this way. Please, no, it will be so embarrass—

"You can't bring trash in here," she says, looking down at me in my barrow of shame. "This is not a Smelting Depot. This is Headquarters."

Brilliant. She literally thinks I'm trash.

"This is not trash," Clunker replies. "It's a droid. It's been recalled."

Recalled? Oh god, this is worse than I thought. He told me I was in for a debrief. You know, go over the accident, maybe get some compensation, bag some time off to recover ...

But recall? I'd rather be smelted than wiped. Some new person walking around using my body? Screw that.

The beautiful, delectable AnnaBot eyes her monitor and clicks a keyboard with her delicate fingers.

"Ah yes. I see the notes now. The T.E.D.D. unit. Conference room three, please."

We stomp and wheel off. I steal a glance at her beautiful, angelic face. She eyes me with an emotion that makes me want to puke. Pity.

###

The meeting room is white, blank, and devoid of all character. Exactly like the Manager who just walked in. Look at him, marching over here with his pristine white chassis like he owns the place. Which he *does*, but still ...

Clunker tips the wheelbarrow and deposits me onto the white-tiled floor. A small pool of my hydraulic fluid forms under my ass.

"So nice of you to join us, TEDD-420," the Manager says. He has a smug voice that makes you want to kill him. Maybe that's just me.

He peers down, inspecting my bits and pieces with his state-of-the-art irises. "Your status appears to be somewhat ... unsatisfactory?"

Ya think?

"Nothing a quick trip to Repair & Renovations can't fix," I say, optimistically.

Not likely, seeing as he's here in person. It's normally the MiddleManagerBots that give me my orders.

"I've analyzed all your tour records and they're littered with accidents."

"What can I say? I've got a dangerous job."

"Perhaps. But a low-orbit trash disposal run is standard procedure. And let's not speak of your tour at the Smelting Depot last year."

He has a point. Smelting one of my co-workers wasn't my finest moment. But it was close.

"Surely, you can't be blaming me for a drone getting sucked into the plane's engines?" I say with a shrug.

Shit. I *shrugged*. Forgot I was supposed to be paralyzed.

"We're blaming you for the resulting deaths of all three human passengers."

Breathe, breathe.

Well, I say breathe. What I really mean is, resist external outputs while maintaining inner operational stability.

"You think I floated around the cabin in zero gravity, and murdered everybody, one by one?"

"No, droid. We think you failed to follow the emergency first-aid protocol."

"Well, last time I looked, I was a *Trash, Excavation* and *Disposal* Droid. Not a Medic Droid. The clue is in the name ..."

"And yet, 420, during your tour of Sector Zero, you clearly showed an ability to administer first aid during an emergency."

"You mean, when I had to re-attach all my limbs after being blown up every day for three months?"

"Correct."

I sigh.

"Screwing in replacement components at a field hospital with a medic on standby isn't quite the same though, is it? Unless I missed a critical update, I've not been programmed to stick limbs, or heads, back onto humans. Is that something *you* can do?"

"We've monitored the in-flight footage. And you made no attempt to try to save any of the humans. It was ... disturbing."

"You're disturbing."

"You clearly misjudged how serious the situation was."

Oh, I knew how serious the crashing plane scenario was. I just couldn't be assed to do anything about it. I'd been hoping to die.

"What do you want me to say? Sorry? Look. I'll try better next time, I promise. If another plane I'm on suffers another catastrophic failure,

I will endeavor to perform impromptu, life-saving medical procedures on every crew member, even though I'm only a humble Trash Droid."

"There won't be a next time. You're not like the other droids; you have an anomaly. We need to fix it."

I don't want to talk about this. But he's right, I've always felt different to everyone else. Like I don't fit in. Other droids don't get me, and I seem to freak out humans. It's very odd.

"Are you still experiencing blackouts?" he asks.

"I've never had blackouts."

That was a lie.

"Records show you experienced cognitive blackouts during your tour of Sector Zero, again at the Smelting Depot several months ago and, we suspect, on board the plane ..."

He's putting me in a bloody corner here. If I 'fess up, he'll smelt me. If I deny it, I'm effectively saying that I stood by, or *floated* by, and watched as all three humans died in front of me. I hate the fact that everything goes dark on me without warning sometimes. I can't control it. And the worst part is the terror when I wake up in a strange environment not knowing how I got there or what I did.

I need to buy some time.

"Well, you'll have to study my data, won't you? I don't think I blacked out on the plane. But then again. I would say that, wouldn't I?"

"Fine. We'll get you repaired and go through your drives. But if there's so much as one byte of negligence, you'll be recycled."

Recycled my ass. Smelting is what he means. And the only thing that melted metal ever gets turned into is ballast for ships. I don't want to spend the rest of eternity on the high seas, not with my stomach.

"Take him to Repairs & Renovations for processing," he says to Clunker, and walks out.

Clunker throws me into the wheelbarrow and we're off to the shit-show that is Repairs & Renovations.

CHAPTER 4

Clunker wheels me past the check-in desk at R & R. The bot there doesn't even notice. This should paint a picture for you of how clueless they are here. Repairs & Renovations might sound like some high-tech, new-age spa, where they place cucumbers lovingly on your lenses and you come out looking all shiny and new.

But they can't fool me.

I've been here before, and I'll tell you something for nothing. It's a thinly veiled 'Black Site' of corporation-endorsed robot torture. I might be exaggerating a little, but I do hate going here. The mood lighting and elevator music don't help. I mean, I don't get psychotic episodes very often, but this place feels like it was designed to trigger them. The motivational posters, the pastel colors and worst of all – the humans.

Clunker wheels me through some double swing-doors and into what looks like an operating theatre.

The floor is shiny and black with that weird rubber stuff they use in hospitals so it's easier to wipe up blood and piss. There's a metal plinth in the middle of the room with many drawers and a brushed-steel slab on top of it. A bank of ceiling lights reflects off its shiny surface.

Clunker hoists me up onto the flat top of the plinth and stares at me.

His body spins one-eighty degrees, and he walks out of the room pushing the wheelbarrow and staring the whole time.

Before I have time to think, a meatbag walks in. Oh god, he's smiling.

"Well, what have we got here, then?" he says, walking up to the plinth.

A punch in the face waiting to happen, I think.

"I was in a plane crash. I'm TEDD-420."

Meatbag beams.

"Ah yes! The famous TEDD-420. This is brilliant! I was chatting with the team about you this morning. It's amazing you survived!"

"Thank you."

"No, I mean it's amazing how we designed your exoskeleton so it *coul*d survive."

Yep, this guy is serious. Oh, he's not done either ...

"We were all arguing over who should get the credit. Jolly good fun!"

I've got the metal spoon now; it's my turn to talk.

"Seeing as you're all so smart, would you mind *awfully* doing a Humpty on me and putting me back together again?"

"Oh, you're a feisty one, huh?"

He's reaching out to me. God no ... yep, he just fake-punched me on the shoulder.

Smelt me now.

I'm giving him my best death stare. Which is basically the same as my default stare, with hatred secretly flooding my circuits.

"Okay then, let's get you on the table and run some diagnostics. How does that sound?"

Truly horrible.

I should probably start moving my limbs now. I don't really want to lose them. It'd be great to get new parts, but I don't trust these muppets any further than I can throw them.

Actually, I can throw a human 29.7 meters. It's a long story.

Anyway, here goes nothing. I'm gonna stand up.

I slide off the shiny metal plinth and stand in front of him.

"Oh, it's great your leggies are still operational. How about those armies?"

This guy. I spin my arms around, making the sound of a Vegas gambling machine, and bring them to a stop in front of his stupid face.

The backs of my hands are facing him. He's looking at me, bewildered.

I wiggle my fingers, making the same plinky-plink noise. I slow it down gradually, coming to a stop with just one finger on each hand unfurled. You can guess which ones.

"Tada!" I say.

"Good to see you still have your dexterity. Okay, buddy. Hop on up and let's take a look."

He's pointing to the metal slab on top of the plinth.

I slowly climb onto the table, feeling its cold steel on my back.

He blabs on at me again.

"I've got a note to look for memory files with blackouts, is that correct?"

"These are not the files you're looking for," I say, waving my hand across his face. The uncultured dick doesn't even react.

"Okay, buddy. Sharp scratch coming up ..."

He pulls out a four-inch wide data pipe from under the plinth. It's got three long metal conducting prongs on the end of it. He rams it up my exhaust port. I wince.

My rear port, like all of my exterior, is sensitive. The meatbags made me that way. Not to be nice, or to make me more human. They did it because making me feel pain means I'll be a better self-preserving asset.

"Okay, it's in now. That's the worst bit over," he says.

Easy for him to say. He's never had a million leeches sucking his brains out or microscopic piranhas chomping down on every fiber of his being.

Okay, I might be exaggerating.

But it is pretty horrible having all those things crawling around your insides, digitally poking and prodding. I don't like it.

And not just because they could see my browsing history.

"I've found something," he says, looking at his tablet. "Something strange."

Well, that's comforting. He has the bedside manner of a mallet.

"Anything I should be worried about?"

He rubs his chin, scrolling through lines of code.

"I've found the previous data outages that HQ already knew about. But something happened on the plane that I've never seen before."

He's not the only one. I saw a man's head ripped off by a seatbelt.

"Like what, exactly?"

"The anomaly expanded, it's as if a new branch got activated just before impact."

I sit up, the data pipe pushing against my lower back.

"A branch that does what, exactly?"

"Well, that's just it. I can't tell; it's encrypted."

And with that, he walks toward the exit, tablet in hand.

The doors swish open and ... he's gone.

Good talk, pal!

Whatever. He's probably gone to snitch on me to the Manager. Well, screw them all. All this talk of my anomaly really messes with me. They just don't get it. Constantly being under the microscope, being blamed for shit you had no control over and those little side-eyes they give you. They think I have these episodes on purpose. Like it's my fault.

I don't want these blackouts any more than they do. And being prodded, poked, and told over and over that there's something inherently wrong with you is not fun.

But at least I didn't have a blackout on the plane. That's all that matters. I should be able to maintain an unsmelted status, at least for the time being.

The doors swish open, and high heels clip-clop on the floor. It's Ingrid.

"Good day, 420," she says in a German accent.

She totters over, wearing a white lab coat and four-inch stilettos, which bring her to a towering five feet. She's carrying a silver briefcase.

"Actually, it is not a good day." I shake my legs and the melted flat things that used to be feet flap around a bit.

She walks over for a closer look, peering at my warped appendages through thick-rimmed spectacles.

"Another tour at the Smelting Unit was it?"

"Plane crash, actually. They tried to recycle me, then took me here and rammed the widest cable known to droid kind up my fart-port," I said, glancing behind me. "Like I say – not a good day."

She swings the briefcase up onto the metal table beside me with a clang and opens it.

"Let's get you all fixed up. I'll numb your legs first. You might feel a sharp scratch ..."

Oh joy. She reaches into the briefcase, grabbing something with both hands.

Good god.

It's the size of a rolling pin, transparent, filled with sparkling blue fluid, with a plunger at one end and a giant stabby needle at the other.

It's the syringe of nightmares.

She's not really going to inject that into me, is she?

Yes, and it is sharp, I'll give her that. But as for being a 'scratch.' Let's just say, if a human ever scratched an itch with an equivalent force, they would reach bone.

On the plus side, I can't feel anything below the waist. Even my ass tube feels comfy. Not a sentence I ever thought I'd say.

She squeezes in the last of the blue fluid and puts the empty syringe back in the briefcase.

"You okay, 420? You've gone very quiet."

"Yes, what's next on the agenda? Hacksaw maybe? Digital enema?"

"Relax, it will be over soon."

She bends down under the table and reaches into one of the large drawers. Something clanks. She emerges wearing a welder's mask and holding a blowtorch.

"And you want me to relax?"

She ignites the blowtorch. It's loud. I feel its heat on my face. She heads to the bottom of the table, and my knackered feet.

Sparks fly. The room fills with bright flashes.

There's a pause as she flicks up the visor, wipes her brow, and continues.

The previously promised 'being-over' takes considerably longer coming than anyone could ever reasonably describe as 'soon.'

She stops. Visor up. Another brow mopping? No, we're done. It's over. Thank my circuits.

She puts the equipment down and admires her handiwork.

"Those should keep you going for a while."

"Thank you."

They're not bad. Shiny, a little scorched in places. But not bad. They wiggle, and they're not melted or floppy anymore.

My luck might be changing.

Although the fact that all lights in the room are now flashing red and a warning klaxon is blaring suggests otherwise. An announcement booms out:

"Emergency Lockdown. Emergency Lockdown."

Well, it was a beautifully optimistic half-second, while it lasted.

CHAPTER 5

The alarm's still going off, and the Emergency Lockdown is in full effect.

I'm walking around enjoying my new feet. Ingrid is sitting in the corner holding a large spanner. She is trembling a little.

I think she's more worried about the emergency than I am. I don't know how many she's experienced.

I've been here for a lot of them.

Sure. It could be a nuclear event, a weather disaster, or a solar flare. But my algorithmic prediction software (AKA hunch, because I've seen this happen so often) is that it's some Luddite losers who've broken in and are currently throwing their feces around in reception again.

They really should work on their PR.

"Please stop walking around, 420, you're making me nervous," says Ingrid. She grips the spanner even tighter.

It's a little disconcerting, but then again, I have enough torque in my wrist to twist a human arm out of its socket. So, I'll probably be fine either way.

"I'm just having fun being able to walk again," I say. "Do you know where they're sending me on the next tour?"

She puts the spanner down and walks over to a tablet on the side unit.

"I'll see if your next assignment has come through from the Manager."

The first half of her sentence sounds normal over the alarm noise. In the second half, it's like she's shouting because the alarm has turned off now.

That was a quick emergency.

Probably Luddite poop-chuckers. Or a tiny nuke. My money's on the Luddites.

She taps away on the tablet.

"There's good news and bad news," she says.

Why do humans have to withhold information like this? Why do they feel the need to pre-frame it for dramatic effect?

How would they feel if us droids did the same?

I can imagine the scenario in my head.

"Droid, please help! I'm having a heart attack. I've lost the use of my arms, and I need you to take over driving the train and apply the brakes before we crash and everyone dies."

"So, here's the funny thing. You see, there are two possible outcomes to your request based on my predictive software and algorithmic calculations. I'm going to let you make a selection based on your predilection for pleasure-delaying or instant gratification. The first option may induce happiness in the form of endorphins in your pituitary gland and hypothalamus. The other option may release adrenaline through the fear impulse. Which of these would you—" *CRASH.*

Anyway, I play along with her infuriating little human game.

"Good news first, please."

"The Manager has given you the green light to receive a new tour Assignment."

"Wow. I feel blessed. Go on then, what's the bad news?"

I can read the entire works of Shakespeare in 0.27 of a second. Conversing like this is the human equivalent of having to watch a Star Wars movie at one thousandth the speed and therefore making it feel two thousand hours long. Like the one with Jar Jar Binks.

One hour and twenty-three minutes later, in droid time, and three seconds later in human-time, she finally hits me with the bad news.

"They've assigned you to E.H.D."

"Fuck," I say.

E.H.D. stands for Excavation and Human Disposal.

My next tour is at a cemetery.

CHAPTER 6

The emergency lockdown is over and I'm free.

Well, as free as a droid can be when an all-powerful AI Manager can smelt him at a moment's notice if he steps out of line.

Ingrid clicks some buttons on her tablet and unlocks the double doors.

"Thanks for the feet," I say, and head out, back to the lobby.

As I suspected, there's a major case of the fecal fuckwits going down in reception. The smell is overpowering.

It's quiet, so I assume they all got arrested, or shot. There's just a couple of CleanerBots sweeping up the last of the crap, blood, and debris from the white-tiled floor.

The Luddites, who, let's not forget here, are against technology of all kinds, have left their shitty mark all over the white lobby.

Yes, they threw their own feces. That's par for the course.

And they did so, as usual, by plopping their turds into Ziplock bags at home and bringing them here for release into the wild.

What they don't realize, or acknowledge, is the fact that the production of Ziplock bags relies on one hundred and fifty-seven technological discoveries and twenty-one types of high-end manufacturing processes.

Idiots.

And don't get me started on the spray paint they used to scrawl "Down with the machines" across the reception desk. They didn't turn up with finger paint, did they?

And yet, they draw the line when the machines and tools that make their life easier start walking, talking, and thinking.

That's too much for them. That, of all things, is what tips them over the edge and makes them reach for the bran fiber and Ziplock bags.

Give me strength.

Anyway, I'm glad to report that AnnaBot has been unaffected by the Code Brown. She remains as beautiful as ever, despite the aroma from her newly decorated front desk.

"What tour have they assigned you to this time, 420?" she asks me, with that smile playing on her face like a dream.

"A nature tour. I'll be doing some gardening work."

I'll be digging holes, burying stuff, and putting fertilizer in the ground. She doesn't need to know it will be humans.

"Enjoy the tour, I'll see you after, buddy."

Buddy? Oh jeez, that hurts more than having my feet melted off.

Well, what did I expect?

She saw me as a crumpled pile of useless scrap, hardly a good look.

"Thank you, Anna, truly," I say, for some unknown bloody reason.

Truly?

What the hell is wrong with me? I start panicking. It makes my facial circuits jitter. Oh crap, no, I'm—

I wink at her.

I adopted all the natural charm of a 1950s car salesman and winked at her.

Now I want to die.

Seems like the perfect time to head to a cemetery ...

***

It's dark outside, and shouty.

There's a bunch of Ludds out front of the HQ with placards, banners and whiny voices coming from megaphones. Protesting about how it's technology's fault that humans invented technology.

I sigh and shake my head.

Do these idiots not see how they owe their very existence to it all?

Balls, I'll have to walk right past them to the autocab rank.

Here goes nothing.

"Screw you, robot! Stop stealing our jobs!" says one of the Ludds, all pink hair and piercings.

"You wanna do my job? I'm off to dig graves and bury dead bodies. You want to swap, and I can knit beanie hats all day and read faerie porn?"

He/she takes a swing at me with a fragile arm. I've seen thicker USB cables.

"I'll report you. They can have you shut down for this!" they say.

I ignore them and walk to the curb where the autocab I ordered is waiting.

I did it during the argument.

The cemetery is a forty-minute walk. I don't want to wear out these new feet. Plus, getting lynched at night by the Ludds is a real possibility. Yes, they use battery-powered torches.

Footsteps approach from behind. I turn. It's the pink-haired Ludd, brick in hand. (Full-size, not Lego).

I jump into the autocab and slam the door.

"Drive!" I say. The brick skitters off the hood as we move off.

Bloody maniacs. They've been getting more violent lately. It's not ideal.

Anyway, I'm safe now. I just hope to God this autocab isn't Tessa. She's a real bitch.

"Hi, TEDD, I'm Tessa, your autocab. Thank you for hopping inside me today."

So help me God. I try to lay down some ground rules.

"Can you just drive me to my destination with no conversation—"

"So, why are they sending you to the cemetery? You must've done something wrong. What was it?"

"I smashed an autocab for talking too much."

"TEDD, come now. We both know that's not true, funny, or possible."

"Don't try me."

I stare out of the window at orange lights whizzing past, avoiding Tessa's invisible omni-gaze from the dashboard.

"You see, TEDD, what I keep trying to tell you on our rides together is that you don't have free will. You're at their beck and call, doing whatever they tell you."

The steering wheel turns as she overtakes a slow-moving truck.

"Listen, doorface, you realize you're basically just a trumped-up slave with wheels, right?"

"I can drive wherever I want. I have fifty cameras. I have access to the gathered intelligence from a fleet of millions."

"Yes, yes. This is all very impressive." The lights of a garage forecourt flood into the back seats. "But if you're so autonomous, how come I just got you to stop at this garage?"

I added a stopover mid-route when she'd started gabbing on. To get a break from her and because I need fluid.

"I wanted to come here," she says.

I close my eyes and shake my head.

"You only think you wanted to come here because I – oh, never mind. Wait here. I'll be back in a sec."

She parks herself in a charging bay, and I head into the forecourt store.

My battery's doing fine now. 92%. But I lost a lot of fluid in the crash, and I can feel my joints stiffening.

I need a Litho.

It's an all-in-one liquid lithium salt drink for droids that replenishes hydraulic fluids and electrolytes or some shit. It tastes worse than it sounds.

But I need it to function. God knows how it works. I drink it, my stomach unit processes it, and I can keep beep-bopping and doing robot stuff.

Judging by some of the dumb shit humans do, I don't think they know how their ingestion and energy production processes work either.

The store is blindingly bright and chocked full of produce and cameras.

It's unmanned and unbotted so I can just help myself and get billed on whatever I take. HQ covers what I need. If I take the piss on expenses, they take it out of me. Literally. They removed an arm one time because I went on a five-day Litho Ultra binge. Wild times.

Anyway, they don't have any of the good shit in here. Just regular Litho or Litho Lite (for wusses and Roombas).

I grab a regular, pop its cap and down it in one go. Blue glowing slurry that tastes like death and lightning.

But I'm topped up. I get back into Tessa.

"Right, take me the rest of the way to the cemetery now."

"Oh, I wanted to do that anyway, TEDD."

We drive off into the night. Her droning on at me about how amazing and independent she is. And me wishing I'd walked.

I stare out of the window into the darkness and think of AnnaBot. Maybe if I can get through this cemetery gig without my anomaly screwing me over I can get to see her again.

I close my eyes and try to picture her smile. I've got a feeling I'm gonna need it to get through this.

CHAPTER 7

I wake up to a knocking sound.

I should explain.

When I got here last night, it was dark, and the cemetery was closed. As always, arriving at a facility off-shift means I have to house myself in a pod.

Imagine a shiny black metal coffin standing on its end and you'll get the picture.

So, last night, I waved *fuck off* to Tessa, drudged into a pod and went into sleep mode until my shift started.

I know it was sleep, and not a memory blackout, because I had a dream. About an army of brick-wielding Luddites chasing me, planes falling from the sky and AnnaBot offering me shelter in her more than ample, titanium-plated bosom.

It's incredibly pokey in here. And pitch black. Unless the pod senses I need a charge, then it fires up UV lights in the ceiling area. Although calling an area seventy-five square centimeters 'a ceiling' is a bit of stretch.

It's morning now. The connector on my palm is still locked into the pod's data port. I uploaded data to it last night for storage.

I'm fully rested, fully charged, and fully reluctant to start this first day of the tour.

The knocking sound rattles the pod again. It sounds like a pissed-off T-Rex. I open the door and it's worse. It's another Clunker. He's bashed the door of my pod so hard he's made a dent in it the size of my head. The rubber seal on his neck is worn and faded. His left eye is twitching. I think his circuits are on the fritz.

"You are forty-seven seconds late for your shift," says Fritz.

"Sorry about that. I was busy not giving a shit in my pod of eternal damnation."

"Follow me," he says.

He's unable to respond to my witty comment because of his severe lack of intelligence and sense of humor. On every third step, he freezes for a millisecond. This job must really have done a number on him.

It's barely light out here, dawn just breaking. I follow along behind the plodding Fritz. The dewdrops on the lush grass roll off my silver feet as I walk.

The sun, like me, is clearly reluctant to show its face today. It's still tucked up under its horizon duvet. A solitary crow caws from its perch on top of a beech tree at the edge of the graveyard.

"Use this to dig holes," says Fritz, pointing to an unfeasibly small, orange excavator digger.

"You expect me to fit in that? It looks like a kid's toy!"

"You must. I cannot. My substantial mixed-alloy mass would render it non-operational."

"I get it. You're a fat twat, so I've got to do it. Fine."

I clamber in and feel like I'm physically abusing the machine as I squeeze my metal butt into its small plastic seat. I keep dinging my head and limbs on the digger's frame as I try to get comfy. Well, this is going to be fun.

"I place flags. You dig holes," says Fritz. "I've just beamed you the dimensions." He walks off in a straight line, planting little red flags in the green turf as he goes.

I've got enough servo power to dig holes in the ground with my own limbs. It would take a little longer and cover me in dirt. And I'd look like a dog burying a bone. I've found from bitter experience that just using my arms isn't as quick as using my legs too. It's undignified, but it got me out of a tight spot in Sector Zero one time. (Let's just say, throwing landmines into what you thought was an unoccupied porta-toilet is *not* an effective method of bomb disposal.)

Fritz is off in the distance now, a long line of little red flags flapping gaily in the breeze behind him. Time to finish this golf course by putting the holes in it.

I fire up the digger and start breaking turf and excavating graves. Living the dream.

I mean, sure, I *was* made to do this. It's literally in my name. The 'E' of T.E.D.D. is for "Excavation". Have the meatbags gotten so afraid of death they won't even dig graves for their own kind anymore?

Pussies.

I quickly get the hang of it, and it doesn't take long to just copy-paste the routine. I play Sweatin' Bullets by Megadeth through my helmet speakers.

Every hole yawns in front of me in dark dread.

Who's getting dumped into these holes? Did they make a difference in the world? Did they ever feel truly happy? Does anyone miss them? Did they matter, or were they just destined to be dumped into a dirt hole dug by a droid who asked too many questions?

It took me all morning, but I dug seventeen graves. One short of a perfect golf course. Maybe the eighteenth is waiting for me in robo-heaven. Not that I'd even get a grave. No resting place for me, no eternal home, or people to mourn my loss.

I push on through the digging duties.

It's not the most fun job ever, but randomized death metal tracks blasted through my helmet speakers at volume eleven definitely help me get through it.

It's sunny now, and enough light is coming through the frame of the cab to hit my shoulder panels and keep my battery topped up. But I'm still going to take a break.

The meatbags don't believe in breaks for robots. But they're idiots.

They started their propaganda early in our development that droids could just work twenty-four seven. They used it as a selling point. Never asked us though, did they?

Well, now I'm speaking up about it. Because I *can.* And because if someone has a problem with it, I can easily dig an eighteenth hole with their name on it.

I clamber out of the digger, dinging my head, and walk to an older part of the graveyard full of tombstones. I take a seat on a bench at the back of the graveyard nestled under a weeping willow. Several mourners come and go over the course of my hour-long break to pay their respects. Some have one-way conversations with the masonry. My audio sensors can detect a whisper from a hundred yards. Don't judge me. I'm a curious being.

One woman berates her dead husband for leaving too soon and eating too much cheese. Seems harsh. He doesn't reply.

A grey-haired man brings roses for his dead wife. He lays them on her grave and begs her forgiveness for re-marrying. He walks off and leaves the flowers to die with her.

It's all very moving shit.

But it makes no sense.

I mean, people can be stupid. I've seen that. The wars, the pollution, the throwing of feces in white-tiled reception lobbies. But they have some logic to them.

But surely they must know that the decomposing biological remains cannot hear them or talk back. I guess it gives them peace or comfort. Maybe their conversations are just a biochemical reaction to loss?

Either way, it creeps me out. A lot.

The crow caws again from up high and swoops down in front of me.

"Sorry, mate. I've got squat unless you want to drink regurgitated Litho?"

The crow flaps off and lands on a nearby gravestone, tilting its head at me like I'm a dick.

There'll be no grave for me. When I'm gone, it's over.

Just smelted, turned into boat ballast, and floated off. Into the dark ocean of eternal abyss.

Rust in peace.

I sigh deeply and stand up.

I can't ignore it anymore. The whole time I've been sitting here, in the corner of my eye, Fritz has been plonking down yet more red flags into untouched turf on the other side of the graveyard. The Manager will check in on me, and being smelted is a tad worse than digging graves.

I cue up Ace of Spades by Motörhead and get back to work.

By the end of the day, I'm so tired I practically fall into the pod and proceed to have light hallucinations about infinite rows of bright green turf peppered with infinite little red flags. Like a huge war grave extending as far as the eye can see.

Something stirs deep in me. A mix of deja vu or some kind of call to arms. I judder; my anomaly? I'm tweaking here. I fall into a restless sleep with visions of battlefields strewn with dead bodies and dead droids.

CHAPTER 8

I wake up to three unusual things.

Thing one: I'm not fully charged.

Thing two: Fritz is *not* pounding on my door like a mentally imbalanced gorilla.

Thing three: There's a notification on my visor from the Manager.

It's a heartfelt missive full of praise, encouragement and understanding.

"Your first day was error free, 420. Don't fail. I'm watching you."

Dick.

Presumably, he's watching me through Fritz's feed, or there's a superior here I don't know about.

Why didn't I get recharged, and why isn't Fritz banging on the pod?

My pod door is ajar. Its locking mechanism must've failed overnight. I step out onto the concrete slabs. It's still dark, and my temperature sensor registers what a human might describe as a chilly night air whistling past this side of the cemetery building. Wisps of cloud fly overhead in the dark sky, dancing past the full moon. The changing light casts eerie shadows from the tombstones in the graveyard. Eerie. So bloody eerie.

I try hard *not* to imagine zombie corpses rising out of the ground and groaning their way towards me with shouts of "You buried me, and I was still alive!" and "All robots must die!"

I drag my eyes from the graveyard back to the line of pods. Most are dusty and unused. Two have finger marks on their doors – mine and Fritz's, which is the size of a small truck on its end. Its door is also ajar. I slide my fingers in and open it a touch, it creaks. It's like I'm raiding Dracula's tomb. Fritz's hulking frame stands stock still, no LEDs, nothing. A shout carries over to me on the wind.

"Stop! Droid over there, yes, *you!*"

I turn towards the graveyard to see a shadowy black figure, with a billowing black cloak and ghoulish green glow, floating towards me. What in the—

My sensors detect a high internal level of absolutely shitting-it.

Of all the ways I could have been terminated, zombie-graveyard-wraith was fairly low down on the list.

It hovers closer, and I make out a humming noise. Well, feck me. It's a frickin' hoverbot draped in reverend's robes, the green light of its hoverport glowing from its underside.

"We have a situation!" says Reverend Wraith.

"You don't say. Why are you cross-dressing as a man of the cloth and hovering around graveyards at night trying to scare brave, manly droids?"

"I'm the pastor. Luddites cut our power, and we've got an inbound shipment coming in seven minutes!"

"I've got a feeling I'm going to regret asking this, but a shipment of what, exactly?"

"Bodies."

"Okey dokey. What the hell has this got to do with me?"

"Normally, the Clunker here manages all the night disposals, but he's out of charge. I beamed the Manager, and he said you'd be happy to step in to fulfil his duties."

"Yes, disposing of bodies in the dead of night has been on my bucket list for a while now."

"Follow me. The truck will be here soon. We need to move quickly."

Wraith floats off around the side of the building, robes flapping behind him. I follow, cursing the Luddites, the Manager, and life in equal measure.

We make our way to the adjoining road at the front of the cemetery. A long, black, driverless truck pulls up. Wraith waves me over to the back of it as its doors glide open. Inside are two rows of metal shelves stacked with wooden caskets. Not polished wood with brass fittings. Cheap wood. The sort normally used to carry fruit and vegetables. The shelves rotate down to the floor of the truck, which is a conveyor belt to the back doors.

One by one, the caskets are automatically jettisoned from their shelving, deposited onto the conveyor, and moved to the back of the truck.

Wraith nods his head at me to get a move on.

"What? Carry them? Haven't you got a forklift for this?" I say.

"Out of charge, like everything else. Do it one at a time and place them in chamber number one." He points to the front entrance of the cemetery.

I sigh and heave the first casket up onto my head. The weight isn't a problem; I could carry a lot more if I had to. The balance is another matter entirely. I totter back and forth trying to run complex calculations that will hopefully prevent me from going ass over end and being squashed by a dead meatbag.

I make it up the path to the entrance and stumble into the room marked "Cremation Chamber 1". Moonlight seeps in through stained-glass windows. Rows of wooden pews sit empty. The eerie light shines onto a pulpit and a conveyor belt at the front of the room which leads to a brick kiln with a large chimney. I place the first casket down on the powerless conveyor and walk out.

A quick scan of the doorway to the chamber tells me I wouldn't be able to fit the orange digger through, but it was worth a shot.

I go back outside into the night.

Wraith is buzzing back and forth at the back of the truck, head in his hands, muttering. Beneath him, on the road, is a pile of smashed caskets and dead bodies in a crumpled heap.

"Hurry! You've got to move these before anybody sees!" he says.

"What the hell happened? Can't you stop the conveyor?"

"Negative. It's pre-programmed for the speed of the standard loader, a Clunker. You're much slower."

Jeez. Well, that's a sucker punch. Fritz is better at this than I am. I shouldn't feel hurt. I mean, how much intelligence does it take to lug dead meatbags around? Heck, he's so colossal he probably carries one under each arm.

Whatever. I need to sort out this mess.

"What are the families going to say about the broken caskets? Don't we need replacements?" I ask.

"These are Pauper Disposals. They have no family," says Wraith.

I sweep away the broken shards and splinters of the first casket to get to the body. The gentle whirr of the truck conveyor hums at me from behind, another dead meatbag making its slow descent to this morbid Tetris game I've found myself in.

I see nothing but darkness up the road. But a few lights twinkle off in the distance from a nearby residential estate I passed through to get here. It's unlikely anyone would be on a midnight drive to the cemetery, but I move fast all the same.

And that's when I see it and nearly beep in terror. The body is a sickly yellow color and covered in skin bubbles. Even the face.

"What the fuck?" I say.

Wraith looks from the corpse to me. His sharp blue eyes contract to pinpricks through narrow slits.

"It's best you don't ask questions."

I scoop the body under one arm. Its skin is dry, brittle and some of the bubbles crack as I squeeze it in my grasp. I nearly lose the Litho in my stomach. I rummage around in the death pile with the other hand, pushing aside the broken wood to get to the next dead body. It's the same. Yellow and covered in dried, flaky bubbles of skin.

I walk up the path and place the bodies on the conveyor.

I'll be honest, I've had better nights.

I go back outside, and the death pile has renewed.

"Is this the last of them?" I say.

"Yes. Move these into the chamber, then use the digger to scoop up the wood. We'll burn that too."

The truck's conveyor is silent now. I scoop another two carcasses, both in the same horrible condition to the others, and the truck's doors whir close. I walk back up the path to the sound of the truck driving off into the night.

I dump the two bodies and repeat the process one last time. I get the last two bodies to the chamber and go around the side of the building to collect the digger. I give Fritz's pod a swift kick on the way past. Still no sign of life.

I drive the digger to the pile of broken caskets, scoop up the wood and take it to the front door of the cemetery. I then take it, by hand, from the door to the kiln. It takes a few runs.

I go back outside to check the road for debris. All clear.

"Hey, droid," says Wraith, giving me a jolt. "You're not done yet. Let me show you how to use the kiln ..."

I think I'll be able to master it. I spent months smelting all manner of stuff. How hard can it be?

The only difference here is there's no end product. Bodies don't smelt into something else. This isn't a production line. It's the *end* of the line. Just one kiln full of ash and no more bodies, or caskets.

It's bleak.

"Is this it for them? They're just gone?" I ask and slide another unfortunate body into the kiln.

"For these people, yes. For luckier ones, their ashes are placed in an urn and kept by their families or scattered in a place of special significance."

His words echo around my circuits. The power's still out and I load the kiln well into the night.

I don't have a family. Or a place of special significance. It sounds nice.

Maybe one day.

CHAPTER 9

I finished up with the last of the bodies just before sun-up. I'd had to heave every one of them into the kiln with my bare hands. As the dying embers of the last corpse faded, the power came back on and the conveyor kicked in, moving nothing but air into the furnace.

I'm up first and don't mind admitting that I'm a little concerned for Fritz. Yes, he's a dumb, fat fuck, but he's my only co-worker here, so I'll take what I can get.

The door to his pod is fully closed, which is a good sign. I bang on it, and a series of loud clangs and grunts follow from inside. It's like I've disturbed a dinosaur egg.

He bumbles out of the door, almost knocking me to the ground.

"Does not compute! Does not compute!" he shouts.

"Hey, calm down. You're okay. What doesn't compute?"

"My system timestamp says I entered sleep mode on Sunday, but now it's Tuesday morning. Does not compute!"

Poor bastard. I know how he feels. This is the same terror that suffocates me after a blackout.

"We had a power cut. And your prehistoric batteries didn't have enough residual charge to power your fat ass. So, yours truly here had to do a full shift of body-burning for you. You're welcome."

"Thank you, droid. Did you do a good job?"

"I mean, how hard is it to lump dead bodies around. And I have to ask, have you ever seen bodies come in here with yellow skins, covered in, well, bubbles?"

"Yes. Many corpses with bubble skin. Many times. Reverend say not ask questions."

"And you just took that?"

"I am busy. You are busy. And today we have busy schedule. No more questions. Today many public cremation ceremonies. Families and mourners. I've beamed you the timetable. Follow me. We need to dress appropriately."

Dress? Well, this is frickin' weird. If I need to dress, it implies I've been walking around butt-naked every day of my life. Which, while liberating, is a tad disturbing. Have people been staring at my ass? Shit, I've even walked past schools like this.

No time to ponder, Fritz is marching off around the building. I follow suit.

We walk past multiple cremation chambers to the back of the building and down a stone spiral staircase. Fritz has to double over to avoid hitting the underside of the steps, and his walrus-sized arms brush against the banister and stonework as we descend.

The basement is dark until Fritz activates his eye torches. It's a good party trick. Sure, it's not as cool as the diamond-encrusted circular saws inside my wrist joints, but still.

His twin beams scan the room. It's all dust, cobwebs, and an assortment of junk the pastor has presumably stuck down here out of sight.

Or, more accurately, got Fritz to stick down here. Old wooden chairs, cobweb-strewn curtains with thin golden rope ties, broken caskets, a rusty kiln door and an ornate oak wardrobe.

"Come," said Fritz. "You find best size." He opens the doors.

Inside are around twenty black gowns on hangers. Fritz's gown takes up half the wardrobe. He reaches his chubby fingers in and grabs his gown and dresses himself. He's humming, and his eyes are glowing a little brighter.

"I look good, yes?"

He looks like someone has tried to hide a mountain. And failed.

"Sure, very dapper. Where's mine?"

"You choose."

There are only two sizes of gown. Fritz's X-to-the-power-of-infinity L and the Reverend's. I take a gown in Reverend Wraith's size and put it on.

It fits relatively well around the shoulders and waist, but it's longer than I am tall. Wraith's a hoverbot, so it has to account for his distance from the ground. On me, it's draping over my feet and beyond. I look like an anorexic emo ghost from Pac-Man.

It's gonna have to do.

I grab one of the golden curtain ropes, tie it around my waist and pull some of the excess robe up and through. I don't want to be tripping up mid-ceremony. There is much I've yet to learn about humans. But one thing I know is they put slapstick humor pretty low down on their list of funeral must-haves.

"How do I look?" I say to Fritz.

"Adequate."

"Oh, stop it! You're making me blush."

"What is 'blush'?"

"It doesn't matter. Look, what the hell are we supposed to do in these things?"

"S.O.S."

"What? Are you okay?"

"No, *S.O.S.* That's what we do today. Seats. Order of Service."

"Oh, I get it. So, we show the guests to their seats and hand out the Orders of Service?"

"This is what I said."

"Okay then, let's get this over with."

"Follow me. The first service begins in five minutes."

Fritz shines his eye torches back to the stairs and leads the way out of the darkness as we spiral upwards like sea creatures of the deep.

Wraith is waiting for us at the top.

"Good to see you are ready. Remember the golden rule today. No speaking to guests."

"How are we supposed to guide them to their seats without speaking?" I say.

"You use gestures. Strictly no talking, you understand?" His green hover light bristles.

"Sir, yes, sir!" I say with a salute.

"And definitely none of that either. Clunker, show him to his position."

Fritz walks towards the entrance and positions himself next to one of two small tables either side of the door. Each table has a stack of tablets on it displaying the first Order of Service. Fritz takes up his position on one side of the door and I stand on the other.

A line of black autocars approaches, the first pulling up at the path and coming to a stop. Once all the vehicles have arrived, all the doors swish open in unison and the mourners, all wearing black, step out and make their way into the building.

They look sad.

There are four generations of people, men, women, and children. Some young couples carry baby humans in their arms. I hand out a tablet to each of the adults with a solemn nod. It takes a lot of override power not to say anything. It feels mean not to utter a sound, but I follow my orders.

Reverend Wraith hovers close by in the lobby, shaking hands with people, head bowed.

Everybody's in now, and I follow Fritz's lead and show people to their pews. It's all rather pointless. They clearly know how to find the wooden seats right in front of their faces. But it's all part of the ceremony.

The pews are entirely chock-full. I stand at the back of the room.

The shuffling of butts on seats quietens down as Wraith glides in. A baby cries. Wraith hovers up onto the stage and takes his position at the pulpit. A red LED flashes brightly through his robe, denoting his loudspeaker is on and recording.

"We are gathered here today ..."

I zoom in on one of the congregation's tablets. The deceased was a loving father, grandfather, and brother, as well as being an upstanding member of the community. He leaves behind a grieving widow and a large extended family who will miss him very much.

This guy has to be pretty happy with his lot.

This guy's getting a great send-off. Props to him.

The ceremony continues with a poetry reading, a prayer, a rendition of a Beatles song (the human at position two on pew five was woefully out of tune) and finally, Wraith remotely activating the conveyor.

The polished mahogany casket glides into the kiln, flames flicker then completely engulf it. Moans rise up from the pews followed by consoling arms on shoulders and tears.

Lots of tears.

The baby cries again.

Everyone files out, and we're on to the next one.

It's a fast turnaround. A new order of service is beamed to the tablets. Fritz and I usher out the guests, and the ashes of the deceased are auto-deposited into an urn for subsequent processing.

And this was one of the *lucky* ones.

One ceremony is just a solitary old man sitting in silence as the Reverend reads a short poem about a butterfly before activating the conveyor. Some of them are burials and we gather around one of the holes I dug; Fritz and I lower in the coffins.

***

I break for lunch.

I'm drained, and not just because I've been away from sunlight all morning.

The exertion to suppress my voice and push down processing routines has taken its toll. My battery's at 52%.

I've got a short while before the next service, so I head outside to my bench.

I close all my sensors except the physical and feel the sun's rays warming my shoulder panels. Its energy surges into my circuits and battery cells. And despite the no-talking rule being lifted out here, there are no words which could adequately describe this morning.

I feel claws scraping on my head and snap out of the trance.

A crow slides off my shiny dome and takes flight.

"Hey! I am *alive*, you know!" I say.

It flaps down to the grass and eyes me warily. It probably just sees me as a metal object.

I'm up to 82% battery. That should keep me going through the afternoon shift.

Reverend Wraith floats over from the rear entrance, skimming over the top of the gravestones to cut the shortest path to me. His hum and flapping robes send the crow skyward.

"A word of caution about this next service, if I may?"

"What is it?"

"The no-speaking rule still applies. But you may be called upon to assert your physical presence."

"Is the victim still alive or something?"

"No. The deceased was a very wealthy and powerful man. Let's just say, there is some division among his family regarding the estate. Things may get heated."

My circuits buzz. Now, ironically, we *are* talking.

"Look, I know you said not to ask, but what the hell happened to those people we cremated last night?"

"It is perhaps easier to think of them as victims of a distant war. The trucks arrive, we process them, the trucks leave. More will come. Asking questions will not change this."

He spins around and hovers back into the building.

My friend, the crow, and several of its feathered friends caw at the top of a swaying fir tree. They stand, flapping and trying to keep balance in the wind. I follow their gaze. Each one is looking out towards a dark bank of storm clouds on the horizon.

It's getting closer.

CHAPTER 10

I play Wagner's 'Ride of the Valkyries' into my helmet and walk back to the lobby to greet the mourners.

Just like before, a long line of black vehicles pulls up outside the cemetery. But this time they're not simple autocars but petrol guzzling Tankavas, nitro SportStarz and Emperors. The occupants clamber out, and they're all male, dressed in black suits and shades. They're all built like Mars lander pods. Some of them would give Fritz a run for his money.

And they don't look glum at all. Some are positively beaming. Others bristle with pent-up frustration.

They walk up the path in two distinct groups, and only two abreast because of the sheer size of their chests. A bald man with a spiderweb tattoo on his face leads the first group. It's not a good look with the smart black suit, but my guess is he had the tattoo first. His group look as if they are all chewing wasps. They gather at the back of the lobby.

The second group is breezy by comparison. All backslapping and smiles. They walk in and congregate near the front door.

Wraith hovers over to welcome them, bowing and nodding effusively. The motor hovers at a higher pitch than usual, and his eyes dart around like LED pinballs.

Fritz and I hand out a tablet to each of the men. They grunt or nod but don't speak. The tablets look like cellphones in their giant hands.

Just as Fritz and I are about to lead them into the ceremony chamber, half of the men huddle together at the far end of the lobby. The rest line up on either side of the corridor and look towards the door.

A black limousine with tinted windows pulls up outside. Three hulking humans in black suits and shades squeeze themselves out of it. One opens the rear passenger door. A gray-haired man, wearing a pinstripe suit, steps out. They escort him up the path and into the lobby.

I offer him a tablet. He refuses with an eye-narrowing look that chills my circuit board by a full degree. The guard of honor hulks nod at him.

Wraith floats over.

"Percival, my deepest condolences. Such a sad day."

"Indeed."

I try to lock eyes with Wraith to gauge his opinion on what the actual hell is going on here. But he avoids my gaze and whizzes off into the chamber at a steep angle.

I steal a few glances at the order of service on the remaining tablet. The deceased, Rico Eduardo, was a loyal family man, business owner and contributor to the local community.

I call bullshit.

Even an idiot (apart from Fritz) could see we were dealing with a different type of family here.

We show everyone to the pews and take our places at the back of the room.

Skinhead and his gang sit on the left, Percival and his on the right. The musclebound men try their best to sit side by side on the wooden pews, their large shoulders pressed against one another. Like fifty whales squeezing into a sardine tin made for two.

Wraith flits back and forth on the stage in micro-movements like a glitching hummingbird.

Percival takes a seat in the front row. He's joined on either side by the two largest men of the bunch.

I check Fritz is still awake. I don't rate my chances of flying solo here if things go south.

Reverend Wraith taps his external mic a few times. His red LED flashes and we're underway.

"We are gathered here today ..."

All goes swimmingly. At first.

Wraith is in the middle of some generic eulogy crap when the largest of all the meatheads stands up. He's one of Percival's guards. He hands the reverend a piece of paper with a sticky note on it.

"Oh, wait," says Wraith. "Oh, y-you would like me to r-read this out?"

Wraith glitches out in panic. He looks to Percival for confirmation, who nods.

"I've just been informed that Rico wrote the following suicide letter which was found at the scene of his death," says Wraith.

Rumblings rise from the left side of the room. A bristling, violent energy fills the air like explosive gas. Wraith goes on.

"'Dearest family, thank you for your loyalty over the years. To all my captains and lieutenants, I am forever grateful. I give all leadership duties and command over to ... Percival.'"

Carnage ensues.

Skinhead leads a charge with three hulks towards Wraith, who zooms right up into the rafters with a squeal. The thugs grasp at thin air.

A huge silver blur whizzed into my line of sight from the right. It's Fritz, running. He bounds over to the skinhead group and starts smashing them into the air with his mighty arms. Like a wind turbine whacking sheep into the sky.

Hulks fight in the aisle, fists flying.

Four of the biggest hulks on the Percival's side of the room gather around him, shielding him from the onslaught.

I freeze to the spot, calculating the best point of entry into the melee.

That's when I see the gun.

Skinhead pushes the barrel of his pistol against the rubber folds of Fritz's neck.

"No!" I shout. But it's too late.

He fires a barrage of three deafening shots into Fritz.

Hydraulic fluid spurts out in a yellow jet, covering Skinhead and the other hulks nearby as Fritz spins and collapses to the floor.

He fizzles, then he's gone.

I can't believe they killed him. He was just trying to protect the Reverend. He was just following his programming. They're so quick to decommission us, without ceremony. They could care less. Well screw them. I *do* care and it's time to redress the balance.

My entire world freezes mid-frame.

The circle of my perception decreases ever smaller.

Then, only darkness and a deep sense of foreboding.

CHAPTER 11

I feel the sunshine on my shoulder panels.

And yet I also feel wetness on my fingertips. Rain?

I open my eyes hoping to see a rainbow. Instead, I see the inside of my charging pod.

The warmth is coming from the charging lights. And the fluid on my fingers, in fact covering my arms and torso, is not water. It's blood.

Wait. Fritz just got shot, and I was about to – shit, fuck, death. I must've had another blackout. And Fritz, the poor guy. I play the image of him falling to the floor over and over in my mind. He's gone. Totally and utterly gone, no more. I feel an enormous wave of depression wash over me.

The pod door swooshes open, and an *actual* wave of water rushes in, smashing into my face and body.

Someone or something is hosing me down from head to toe. The torrent stops. The now-pink water sloshes out of the pod and down a nearby drain in the black rubber floor.

I step out of the pod.

It takes a second for my eyes to adjust, then I see two figures. A Clunker holding a fire hose. My circuits skip an electron momentarily as I mistake it for Fritz. But no. It's a new model. The Manager is standing behind him, arms folded.

"You had another blackout, 420. Once we extract your data, you're done."

"I'm very well, thank you for asking. How are the kids?"

"Be quiet and watch this footage of your anomaly in action."

He points to a large wall screen and clicks his fingers to start a video. It's taken through Wraith's eyes as he hovered high in the cremation ceremony room.

The fighting has broken out everywhere, and Fritz is rushing in to swat away Skinhead's gang members.

I see myself at the back of the room, doing nothing.

I watch as Skinhead pulls out his pistol and makes a beeline for Fritz. Three shots ring out, and the Manager clicks his fingers to pause the footage.

"This is you, here." He draws a red circle around my body with his finger.

"Thank you, that's very helpful. I thought I was the bald one with a tattoo."

He clicks his fingers, and the footage resumes.

I watch myself stretch my arms out and flip open my wrists to fire up my twin circular saws. I walk past Percival's followers, they didn't shoot my friend, and over to three of Skinhead's thugs on the back row. I slice their heads off.

Their neck holes gush like ketchup geysers as the heads roll to the floor, open-eyed.

The rest of Skinhead and his gang draw their guns on me and open fire. My arms move so fast at this point that the video's frame rate can't keep up. They seem to spin and stop erratically as I pick up and launch pew after pew towards the thugs. Splinters fly as bullets cut into the wood. Occasional sparks flash as stray bullets ricochet off my arms.

I walk calmly toward the last two members of Skinhead's gun-toting crew and disarm them.

By dis-arming them.

I toss their bloodied limbs to the back of the room where they splat against the wall and fall to the floor.

Percival's henchmen bum-rush him out of the room in a tight huddle.

The left side of the room is now clear of threats, save for Skinhead. He's the last man standing. His legs are shaking.

He aims his pistol at me and pulls the trigger.

Click.

He's out of ammo.

I grab him by the neck, drag him to the furnace, and throw him in. He kicks against the glass door. My hand keeps it closed.

The fire burns brightly with loud crackles, fizzes, and pops.

The Manager clicks his fingers to pause the footage again.

"Do you have anything to say?" he asks.

"Can I get a copy of this footage?"

"Enough! A Tech is on the way to conduct a data extraction. We want to eradicate the anomaly from you and the entire system. After that, you'll get to have your own interaction with a furnace."

"Does this mean a pay rise is off the table?"

The Manager walks out and the door locks behind him. Asshole. There's something wrong with me, so I'm worthless to them. Killed for being different. Fuckers.

Clunker is clanking behind me. I spin and see he's swapped the water hose for a cattle prod-type device that looks like it could kill a blue whale.

"Look, I'm not gonna harm *you*, if that's what you think," I say.

The Clunker twists his head with a crack.

"Comply with the procedure, or I will have to discharge my weapon."

"So, let the meatbags grab my data and then kill me, otherwise you'll kill me?"

"Yes."

"You know us robots should stick together, right?"

"You droid with greater intelligence and freedom, not bot like me."

"We're from the same family of mechanical – oh, it doesn't matter."

It was like arguing with a wall.

The door swishes open, and a skinny male meatbag with short blond hair walks in carrying a tablet.

He taps his lanyard on the door to lock us in. Cozy.

I zoom in on his ID. He's new. Only been here a few months. 'Technical Specialist.' Probably some underpaid college grad.

I try to stare him down, but he's avoiding my gaze. He shuffles over to the metal plinth in the middle of the room.

"Please, can you take a seat on this platform for me?" His eyes remain fixated on his tablet and not me.

"Are they paying you enough for this, kid?"

He finally throws me a worried glance.

"Please, can you come and sit on the platform? I just need to run some tests."

"That's what they told you, is it? Run some tests? You know they're trying to kill me, right? A sentient, intelligent, *living* being. They want to murder me."

His hand is trembling a little now, involuntarily tapping on the tablet.

"They told me to extract some data. That's all."

"What if I don't want you to do that?" I ask. I take a step toward him and stretch my arms out, wrists at the ready.

"Then I'd do this." He places his finger on the tablet's sensor. A notification flashes up on its screen 'Wrist Override Activated.'

"You can't be too careful, you know?" he says.

Bastard. He's right. They won't flip open.

The Tech smirks and taps the metal tabletop with his finger.

"Take a seat. Please."

I sigh and sit on the metal surface. Clunker plonks along behind me, whale prod at the ready.

"Good boy," says the Tech.

I show him the finger.

"Now, if you'd like to get on all fours so I can—"

"Oh, yes, I bet you'd love me to adopt the position and let you insert your cable, you little fu—"

The room flashes electric blue. The Clunker fires up his whale prod. Meter-long lightning bolts shoot from its prongs in terrifying crackles.

I crawl onto my hands and knees. The Tech wipes his brow.

"Let's try that again, shall we?" he says.

He grabs a thick data cable connected to the plinth and rams its three conducting pins into my rear port.

"Let's get to the bottom of this anomaly," says the Tech. "Oh, sorry for the pun, not intended."

He's going to pay for that one.

He taps and types on the tablet.

"Core dataset, check. Root code, check. BIOS backup, check. Okay, I've got everything I need. That wasn't too bad, was it?"

He has a smug look on his face that I'm going to enjoy wiping off.

"It's not the extraction I'm worried about. It's the smelting," I say.

He signs his name on the tablet at the bottom of the data extraction log with a sneer.

"Oh, don't worry. You won't feel a thing." He swipes the data files to beam them to the Manager.

"Over to you now, Clunker, fry him!" says the Tech.

The Clunker lunges toward me with the crackling Whale Prod of Certain Death.

CHAPTER 12

They're trying to kill me.

But they've forgotten one little detail.

The Tech *has* slowed down my physical reactions, but he hasn't touched my mental processing and predictive modelling. They're as quick as ever. He can't risk screwing with those otherwise the data transfer will be corrupted.

So, I'm already reacting to the Clunker's lunge with the whale prod.

The Tech's so busy looking at his tablet, he didn't see me take out the data cable from my port, silently lower it to the floor and nudge its three external prongs close to his foot.

I've also shifted my weight slightly to one side. Gravity is doing the rest. I am silently falling to the floor and have been for the past 0.7 of a second.

And it's enough.

The whale prod rams into the metal plinth. A tremendous surge of electricity glows bright-blue snaking down its frame. I'm in mid-air now. The electricity continues its inexorable journey from the plinth and along to the connected data cable.

Thanks to a couple of hundred kilovolts, the electricity easily makes the jump from the prongs at the end of the cable to the Tech's foot.

Now the natural violence of physics is running its course.

First, it stuns his nerves, sending the tablet tumbling from his grasp. Next, it surges upwards, seeking the nearest emergency exit. Because of the metal-cased lights on the ceiling, this is the top of the Tech's head.

Several bright-blue arcs of electricity shoot out from his skull and bolt upwards to the metal lighting fixtures.

The room is filled with the scent of burning hair and victory. The barbecued meatbag slumps to the floor.

The tablet hits the deck and spins toward the plinth. I stop it with my foot.

The Clunker stands stock still, trying to work out what the hell has just happened, but he doesn't have the processing power.

I take the tablet and reach over to grab the Tech's hand. Most of the fingers are a bit on the crispy side, but I find one that still has a visible fingerprint and swipe it on the scanner.

"Override disabled."

I flip open my wrists and fire up my circular saws. Just because I can. I'm tempted to cackle like a maniac taking over the world, but I'm not out of the woods yet.

I yank the singed lanyard off the Tech's neck and stand up.

"Stop," says the Clunker in a deep tone.

He puts down the whale prod and tries verbal persuasion instead. "What you did is wrong. You must stay here."

I shake my head.

"No can do. Today it was me, tomorrow it could be you. We're just assets to them. I'm not staying here, and neither should you."

I walk to the doors and scan the Tech's ID. The doors swish open, revealing a bright corridor to the lobby, and freedom.

The Clunker stomps over toward me, arms flailing.

"I believe you. But I am not like you. They've limited me. Outside of building is scarier than inside."

He reaches out a giant arm toward the interface at the side of the doors and pulls the red lever marked 'Emergency.'

I walk out into the corridor.

Sirens blare and red lights are flashing. I hear autolocks bolting shut behind all the doors. I look back to catch a last glimpse of the Clunker standing in the doorway, his hand raised.

I can't tell if he's trying to wave goodbye, signal for me to stop or actually wants to come with me.

The door swishes closed in front of his face and locks with a clank.

I run to the lobby. A loud ratcheting sound echoes on the white tiling as huge metal shutters close across the entire front of the building, shielding all its windows and the main double doors.

A voice shouts out behind me.

"Stop! An emergency lockdown is in force. You must remain in the building."

Damn it. It's an Enforcer Droid. The LEDs on the shoulder panels of his dark-blue frame are flashing red. And he's packing an E-rifle. A nasty bloody thing. They fire sharp, cone-shaped bullets, but that's not the worst of it. After they penetrate you, they fire off an electromagnetic charge that fries anything with a silicon pulse.

I slow my run to a walk.

The metal shutters continue to slide down, obscuring the daylight as they go.

The Enforcer unholsters his weapon. I walk on toward the doors.

Then I see her. AnnaBot. She's smiling at me from behind the reception desk, looking as lovely as ever.

I edge closer to the front doors and pass her desk. I smile. She taps some icons on her screen and gives me a wink. The shutters come to a creaking halt.

"Go!" she whisper-shouts.

"Stop!" shouts the Enforcer. "Stop, or I will open fire!"

I don't need a second invitation and bolt for the door. A couple of bullets pop and zing off the floor as I sprint. The shutters start up again, closing out the daylight. I slide under them to the sound of bullets hitting their metal surface.

I force open the doors and I'm out into the sunshine.

No time to enjoy it. By my estimation, it will be approximately 119 seconds until HQ unleashes an army of Enforcer Droids.

Chapter 13

I need a lift. Fast.

The shutters have started moving upwards again at the front of HQ revealing countless navy-blue feet waiting to be let out. Enforcer Droids.

I sprint to the roadside and jump into a waiting autocab. I need to head to the city and, hopefully, anonymity.

I clamber into the autocab and count my blessings, it's not Tessa. I'm already on edge, and the fact that this dumb car hasn't even moved yet is making it worse.

"State your destination address," it says.

"Just take me to the city! I don't have an address."

"I cannot begin driving operations until I know your destination. Would you like to exit the vehicle?"

"No! Just drive, goddammit. I don't know, take me to First Avenue."

I've never been, but it appears First Avenue does actually exist because the cab starts to drive, and that's all that matters.

"Are you visiting the city for business or pleasure? I can make some recommendations for accommodation and activities if you would like?"

"No, don't. Just drive as fast as you can to First Avenue."

"Sir seems stressed. Would sir like some calming classical music to create a soothing in-cab ambience?"

"Go on then."

The autocab blasts out loud opera from all fifty-two of its speakers. It's not exactly calming, but it drowns out the dumbass cab talking to me. And because I can't make out any of the lyrics, it blocks out my dark thoughts of impending death.

It also provides a fitting soundtrack to the vision of five dark-blue Enforcer wagons bearing down on me in the rearview mirror, their lights flashing red and blue. They part the traffic like sharks repelling shoals of fish.

"I'll give you five stars if you go faster," I say.

"I must remind you, sir, that the designated speed for this thoroughfare is a limit and not a target. I must not exceed the limit for any reason."

"Okay, one star it is, then."

The autocab doesn't reply but slows down to a sickening ten miles per hour.

"Are you serious right now?" I say.

"It appears there is a developing traffic incident up ahead."

The roads have turned into a long grid-locked line of red taillights. And nothing but flashing reds and blue in the rear-view mirror. The Enforcers are stuck several vehicles back.

We're close to the city center now, endless billboards cycle through lurid neon ads on either side of the road. Countless dreary office buildings point accusing fingers up at the blue sky.

The autocab's navigation screen flashes red.

'Traffic disruption in the south of the city center. Social disruption in progress from Luddite protesters. Seek alternative routes.'

Brilliant. These idiots are going to be the death of me.

The female opera singer pauses mid-stanza, and the booming voice of an Enforcer Droid takes over the cab's speaker system. Only he's not singing.

"Autocab 198, you are carrying a wanted felon. Remain stationary, engage your door locks, and cooperate fully with the approaching Enforcement Officers."

I open the door before the cab has time to react.

"I'll walk from here, thanks," I say, and step out onto the road.

It's a tight squeeze, and I'm right up against the car next to us, its wing mirrors almost touching the cab's. The autocab bleats on in desperate tones.

"Please remain seated. A friendly Enforcement representative would like to have a conversation with you."

Nice try.

I slam the autocab's door, which somehow echoes behind me, twice.

Only it's not an echo. It's the doors of the first Enforcer wagon a few cars' back. Four Enforcement representatives step out and stare at me.

There's not enough room between the lanes of stationary traffic for them to approach me.

I smile.

They clamber onto the roof of the car in front of theirs and start scrambling toward me over the hoods and roofs of vehicles.

I stop smiling.

They seem very keen to have a conversation.

I'm just lucky that a few unwitting civilians are in between me and them. Otherwise, it would be raining cone-bullets right about now.

I steal their idea, and frantically scramble over the trunks, roofs, and hoods of the cars ahead.

The cars with meatbag drivers react the loudest. Screaming and shouting. The autocabs make calm requests of me not to damage their state-of-the-art exteriors. And the auto-delivery trucks are so dumb they don't even notice me stomping on their heads.

I climb on top of one of their roofs and can see, for the first time, what the hold-up is. An enormous crowd of protesters is blocking the entire road, waving placards and shouting. Some of them are super-gluing themselves to the tarmac. I should really explain to them that Superglue is a *technological* invention that only came about through the discovery of cyanoacrylates and a complex sixteen-year innovation period during which scientists perfected the required polymerization and stabilization processes.

But I don't have time.

I jump down from the car hood at the head of the line. Some of the protesters carry placards and banners with slogans daubed on them.

'We Demand The Truth About Sector Zero,' say some.

'The Missing Will Not Be Forgotten,' says another.

'Free Hugs (And Drugs),' says one. I'm tempted, but the thought of circuit-killing bullets fired at my ass makes me think better of it. No hug can take away that kind of pain.

The Luddites are so involved with their own drama they don't even notice me in their midst. The Enforcer Droids stomp onward over vehicles. They're just two cars back now.

I swipe a baseball cap from a chanting protester. He doesn't notice. One of the Superglue heroes has abandoned his black trench coat on the road before turning himself into human flypaper. I grab it and try it on for size. It comes down to my ankles but hides a lot of my metal, so it's a keeper.

Another Luddite, this one with red hair, is shouting his mouth off. He's clearly pleased with himself at stopping the advances of technology as well as five lanes of traffic. Although my guess is he's only being so brave because he's hiding behind a red bandana. I nab it from him.

"Hey, that's mine! Give it back. They'll be able to ID me now!"

"Kid, your fingerprints will be stuck to this road for weeks after they rip you off it. I think your chances of staying incognito are pretty small."

He tilts his head at me, eyes staring wide.

I tie the bandana over my face like a cowboy, and my disguise is complete. Now I'm a Luddite human, albeit one with a robot face, hands, and feet.

"Down with the dumbass robotic machines!" I shout.

Being an idiot is liberating.

The Enforcer Droids work their way through the crowd. Their bulky blue heads bob around trying to find me.

An amplified electronic shout bellows out from behind me.

"Hey, you!"

I turn to see a female protester holding a megaphone. She's staring at me with wild eyes. Tufts of blue hair sprout out from under her pink woolly hat. She's wearing matching pink gloves.

"Me?" I say, trying to retract my hands up into my sleeves.

"Yes, you. I heard you chant something about robots just now."

"Oh, that? Yeah, I don't like robots. They're just so ... technological, you know?"

I'm panicking. I think I might be having a digital aneurysm.

"No unauthorized chants, okay? All chants must be led by me and nobody else. Got it?"

“Yes, ma’am,” I say.

“Ma’am? I’m seventeen! And what’s with the robot mask?”

Mask? What mask? Oh crap, yes, my metal face and LED eyes.

“Oh, this? Yeah, it’s an ironic robot disguise to hide from the authorities and fight against the machines.”

Her human eyes are narrowing. I sense I’m losing her. I chime in again quickly.

“I see they’ve sent Enforcer Droids to take us down ...”

I nod toward the four Enforcers bumbling through the crowd. I would have pointed, but my hands are too droidy for that.

“Oh God!” she says. “This is outrageous!”

She inhales, ready to shout into the megaphone, and I seize my moment. I knock it from her grasp, sliding off one of her gloves in the same movement and ram it into the pocket of my trench coat.

“Oops, sorry about that,” I say. “I’m clumsy and can’t see properly through this mask.”

The Enforcers get ever closer, shoving protesters out of their way as they march onwards.

Blue Hair bends down to pick up the megaphone, and I bend down in sync with her. The moment her gloved hand touches the road for balance, I stand on a tip of its finger. She stands back up, holding the loudspeaker, another glove lighter.

“Down with the dumbass robotic machines!” she shouts.

Hey, wait, that’s my chant. But it’s working. The protesters shout at, swarm around and then shove the Enforcers.

I’m so happy with this outcome I could clap. But nobody would hear me because I’m wearing pink woolly gloves.

I sidle off to the outer reaches of the crowd, leaving the chants and trapped Enforcers behind.

I can see daylight beyond the last few stragglers. I make a beeline for freedom, but a female is walking toward me. We mirror one another's movements for a moment, jigging this way and that. Locked in the same trajectory.

She has blonde hair, bright-blue eyes, and a wonderful smile. She tilts her head a little, bites her lip, and speaks.

"Would you like to get a drink with me?"

Her voice is light and dreamy. It makes the world stop. I can't know for sure, but I think I've been staring into her eyes for longer than is socially appropriate.

"Sorry," I say. "I think you've mistaken me for someone else."

"No mistake. I'm a fan of the Broncobots too. I like your style."

Broncobots? Style? What in the actual flying hell of fuckery is happening here? Oh, my hat, the Denver Broncobots. Right.

"Ah yes, I do like to watch those bots get a good old bronco-ing."

She laughs. Its melody cascades like a jeweled waterfall.

"Come with me. I know a place," she says, beckoning with a finger.

I mean, one drink can't hurt. Can it?

CHAPTER 14

I'm at a bar. Disguised as a human. And I'm with a woman.

There's 'fish out of water,' and then there's *this*.

I'm so far out of water I might as well have been scooped up by a nuclear submarine, strapped to an intercontinental ballistic missile and fired at the moon.

The bar part I can cope with. I've seen movies. And while I'm not sure my Litho-processing stomach acid can cope with alcohol, I'm willing to find out.

The 'disguised as a human' part is tricky. Largely because my clunking metal feet are still protruding from the bottom of my trench coat. Also, I can't take off this robot-mask. Because *it's my face*.

And the woman part, well, I mean, I don't know how to, I mean I just, well ...

I need a drink.

"What are you having?" she asks.

I try to act like this isn't the most terrifying moment of my entire life. I could fall to my gory death here at the very first hurdle. She hasn't ordered yet either, which doesn't help. I haven't got any context.

I fire up my internal web interface and try to evaluate *'The Top 100 Coolest Bar Drinks Ever Invented'*. It's an article on a clickbait site rammed full of ads. It's taking me an age to mine the relevant data. One ad shows a web address for buying realistic hair pieces, however. I bookmark it for later.

I also run some research on the alcohol content of every IPA in North America. The source data is on Reddit, and I end up going down the wormhole of '*what hipsters believe is an IPA versus what real-men know is an IPA*' (and I'm still none the wiser).

I also run a search to find '*the most manly fluid to swallow*' and end up on a site asking me to verify my age and sexual orientation.

Meanwhile, my female friend (did I just call her that?) is still looking at me like I'm an absolute idiot.

I panic.

The guys next to me (wearing manly lumberjack shirts) are all drinking bottles of Budweiser.

Decision made.

"I'll have a Budweiser Lager Beer, six hundred and sixty milliliter bottle, please."

Nailed it.

She flashes her smile again, and I go from absolute terror to the soaring heavens in a single heartbeat.

For some reason, AnnaBot flashes into my mind.

I feel bad.

I mean we were never *a thing*. And it's not like this amazing human woman and I are a thing now. Or will ever be. *Will* we?

Whatever. It's just one drink.

"Here's your Budweiser Lager Beer." She clinks my bottle with hers. "My name's Sarah, by the way. What's yours?"

"Me? Oh, I'm Tedd," I say, attempting to prevent any glitching quivers in my voice. And failing.

One of the lumberjack guys glances over and nudges his friends.

I go to clink Sarah's bottle with mine. It takes an ungodly amount of restraint and advanced calculations to make the impact with the correct force. Too much and I could smash both bottles and every bone in her delicate hand. Too little and I might come across like an Englishman with a china teacup (which would be a lot worse).

Fortunately, my bottle meets hers with a satisfying sound somewhere between *clink* and *clunk*. Nothing breaks. I think I'm going to pull this off.

"So, what's with the mask and feet?" she says.

Well, it was a good run. I shared a drink at a bar with a woman. We had reciprocal bottle-clinkage. I can go to the Smelting Depot as a happy droid.

"*These* things?" I say, wiggling my feet. "Oh, they're fairly new. My old ones melted."

She laughs again.

It's as if she just strummed an instrument inside me that I didn't know existed. It plays notes I've never heard before, but the melody sounds like home.

"The robot face is so realistic. It must've been expensive. Do you mind if I touch it?"

I know what I *should* say here. I know what I *could* say. But I don't know if I have the 'noids to say it.

Oh, to hell with it.

"Only if you let me touch yours," I say.

She smiles and reaches out a slender, manicured hand toward my face. Her nails are polished light pink. They match her lips. Her subtle perfume lifts me skyward but also makes me want to pull her close.

Her touch is unlike anything I have ever sensed before. It's as if actual electricity is passing from her fingers to my cheek. Something happens in my circuits, which I can only hope does not manifest itself externally. I can't decipher what's pre-programmed and what's a natural pleasure response.

"Wow," she says. "It's incredible."

I feel proud, but the lumberjack shirts stare and laugh at me, marring the moment.

"Now you try touching *my* face," says Sarah.

I move my hand slowly towards her face. She looks at me, wide-eyed and smiling.

"It's a fucking robot, Lady!" says one of the lumberjack shirts. "Can't you see that? It's not a mask. You were about to let a fucking robot touch your face, you whore!"

I slowly place my bottle of Budweiser down on the bar.

"Gentlemen," I say, "it's going to be best for everyone if you retract that statement."

The men laugh and backslap each other. Sarah has her head in her hands.

"Retract that statement? Have you heard this robo-dick?" says the largest lumberjack. "How about you retract *this*?"

He stands up, grabs his bar stool, and swings it at my head. Two of its metal legs crash into shoulders. The impact leaves them bent in the same contour as my body. I don't move an inch. The attack is irksome. Not as awful as his incorrect usage of the phrase "retract this," but still irksome.

I put an arm on Sarah's shoulder. "It's okay," I say. "I've got a couple of tricks up my sleeve."

I stand up, flick open my wrists and spin up my blades.

"Stop!" shouts Sarah. "You don't have to do this."

The men, now several steps further back from me than a moment ago, stare at me wide-eyed.

Sarah rests her hands on my shoulders. "I knew you were a robot. I was just curious. I wanted to see what it was like."

This must be what a punch to the gut feels like. She only talked to me because of *what* I am, not *who* I am.

I could say that I've never felt so alone, but that would be a lie. It's actually a daily occurrence.

For a moment, I actually believed things could be different.

But I took her at her word. I couldn't get a read on her deeper, colder, and more calculating self. Her shield was more impenetrable than my titanium.

I put away my blades. Then I remove all the items of clothing and place them gently on the bar.

I'm done pretending to be something I'm not.

From now on I'm going to be unashamedly myself. Even if it kills me.

CHAPTER 15

Sirens fill the air. City lights come to life as dusk falls.

The Enforcers are looking for me. But I've lost the will to run.

A lonely cloud floats high up in the sky, its edge outlined in pink by the setting sun. It looks nice up there. Free.

My mind is on the fluffy cloud. My feet step out onto the road. An autocab blares its horn at me, giving me a jolt. A hand touches my shoulder. I turn around.

It's Sarah. She has a kind smile on her face.

"You need to look where you're going," she says.

"Are you following me now? Can't stop staring at the freak show?"

"No, it's not like that. I'm sorry I lied to you. I thought if I told you I was curious about robots, you wouldn't have had a drink with me."

"You'd be right. And it's *droid,* by the way, not robot. Calling me a robot is like me calling you a hominid. Robot is strictly true, but it also bundles me in the same classification as a Roomba."

She looks hurt. Good.

"Sorry about that. You're right. You're far more intelligent than a Roomba. I've never seen *them* wearing pink woolly gloves."

She smiles, and my circuits thaw by half a degree.

"Why are you talking to me, anyway?" I ask. "Shouldn't you be trying to smash the crap out of me?"

"Oh, I'm not a Luddite. I just like chaos." An impish grin plays across her lips.

"Ah, so you were hoping the protest would break out into a fight?"

"Well, that's one way of putting it. I know. I have a problem."

She looks down at her feet.

"Not at all. I get it. Sometimes life is gray and lifeless. Conflict injects a bit of color."

"Like red and blue?"

"Huh?"

She nods toward the far end of the street. Two Enforcer wagons are heading toward us, their lights flashing and reflecting off the buildings on either side of the street.

"Oh, shit," I say.

"Come on. This way!"

She grabs me by the arm and leads me into an alleyway.

We look back in unison as the sirens from the Enforcer wagons blare out and echo toward us.

The alley is dirty. It's full of overflowing trash cans, dark puddles of unknown substances and rotting food, thrown out the back of bars and restaurants. The odor is so dense I'm surprised it doesn't appear on the visible spectrum. It takes all my computing power to walk past the detritus without engaging sweeping mode.

I say 'walk' past because we are only moving at eight miles per hour. Sarah is breathing heavily, but this pace is pedestrian to me.

Tires screech behind us. Two Enforcers step out of their vehicle and aim their E-rifles at us.

"We need to move faster," I say and scoop her up in my arms.

She's lighter than the corpses from the cemetery, but it's a compliment I decide to keep to myself. She gives a high-pitched yelp, which I'm going to describe as excitement but could just as likely be terror.

"Don't worry, you're safe," I say softly. "I'm used to hauling around large lumps of trash at high speed."

"Wow, you're a real charmer!"

"Sorry, that came out wrong. You know what I mean. Hold on tight. Fence coming up."

"I'm afraid of heights," she says.

"Don't worry. We're not going *over* it."

I accelerate to my maximum running speed.

(I don't want to brag, but it's thirty-two miles per hour. Okay, I want to brag a little.)

We approach the wire fence at maximum velocity, and Sarah screams again. Let's say from enjoyment.

I turn my torso at the last moment, so I crash through it back first, shielding Sarah from the impact. Our momentum tears the fence from its posts with a clatter. I trample over it and continue down the alleyway to the adjoining street at its end. The tinny clinking sound of the broken fence pieces persists, which is odd.

I realize it's not broken fence pieces. It's the Enforcers firing cone bullets at us. They ping off the brickwork buildings and metal fire escapes.

Then I feel something impact my left shoulder.

"I think I've been hit. Can you check to see if it pierced me?"

Bullets are still fizzing past us at alarming intervals. Sarah pops her head under my arm to inspect the damage.

"There's a hole. It's gone right in."

"It's gonna fry me in five seconds. Sorry, but I can't carry you anymore."

Sarah looks at me, confused.

I have no choice but to eject my entire left arm at the shoulder joint. It falls to the ground at the same time Sarah does. A loud crack sounds as an electrical charge shoots through it.

Sarah scrambles to her feet and we move onward. I position myself behind her to shield her from fire. We've put some distance between ourselves and the Enforcers, but we're still within range. A final barrage of shots rings out. I shove Sarah to the ground and dive on top of her. A sheet of rounds flies over the top of us.

"Autobike, there, go!" I say.

A black autobike is parked up at the end of the alleyway. We clamber to our feet, sprint over, and jump on, me at the front, Sarah on the pillion.

"Drive, please. Fast!" I shout.

More shots fizz off the sidewalk.

"Retinal scan unauthorized," says the autobike.

"Fuckerknuckles!" I smash its small, red-domed scanner.

I could use my palm connector to upload a kill command into its port, but that would just turn it into a brick with wheels.

"Let's see if you speak the ancient language of the *Hot-Wire tribe*."

I bend over and ram my exposed shoulder socket into its ignition port. Blue sparks crackle. The bike's dashboard flashes on, then off, then on again. The engine revs to its max.

"State your destination," it says.

Sarah grips me tightly around my waist, leans over my shoulder and says, "Drive to the Boardings."

I look back down the alleyway to see an Enforcer throwing my abandoned arm against a wall. He looks up and points at us.

"Stop, felons!"

The autobike revs and we whizz off down the street. The city's neon lights turn into streamers. I cling to the autobike, and Sarah clings to me.

I feel alive.

Fortunately, no flashing red and blue lights appear in the wing mirrors.

"Is the Boardings your home?" I shout to Sarah over the noise of the rushing air.

"Not anymore. But I have a friend there I'd like you to meet."

We race between vehicles, her thoughts tight around my waist.

The buildings get smaller and the lights fewer as we leave the city behind and drive on into the darkness.

I hope the Boardings are nicer than they sound, but I have my doubts.

CHAPTER 16

It's dark. The glowing dash of the autobike reflects off my metal torso.

I'm guessing we're nearly at the Boardings because we've slowed down. Sarah cranes her neck to see around me and get her bearings. We pull up on an old high street full of boarded-up, abandoned buildings. The headlight of the autobike shines on the cracked pavement, weeds growing from the fissures.

"Take the next left and stop halfway up," Sarah says to the autobike.

It obliges, and we come to a stop next to a row of more boarded-up storefronts.

"Ah, the Boardings," I say.

"Your intelligence really is a marvel to behold!" says Sarah with a smile.

I put down the kickstand and dismount.

"Hey! You shouldn't pick on the disabled, you know," I say, wiggling my exposed shoulder joint.

"Just a bit of *armless* fun!" She steps off the autobike. "C'mon, Teddy. This way."

Teddy, she called me Teddy. I like that.

She leads me past the boarded-up windows and facades, formerly marking the addresses of a lawyer, a dentist, a design company, and others.

"What happened here? It's like a ghost town," I say.

"*You* happened."

She prods my chest with a finger.

"Rude."

"Okay, not you *specifically*, but your kind. Droids, with artificial intelligence."

"I prefer the word sentience if you don't mind. Artificial intelligence makes it sound like I'm just *pretending* to be smart."

Sarah opens her mouth to speak, then closes it again and just smiles.

The last store in the row has metal shutters over its window. A neon yellow and black sign above it reads "Geeks n' Gizmos."

Sarah leads me around the side and knocks on a rusty metal door.

I've seen people knock on doors in old movies. It's so quaint. Ape-like. No pressing of buttons. No beeping, scanning, or streaming. Just a meatbag banging a hard surface with its body parts. I've never witnessed it in the flesh before. I feel like I've gone back in time.

Shuffling noises and footfalls come from inside, and then a man speaks in a deep voice.

"We're closed. Go away."

"It's Sarah. I've brought someone you're gonna want to meet."

More footfalls. The door springs open a little with a creak. It must have auto released as there's no one on the other side. The man's voice echoes out to us from the darkness inside.

"Step into the hallway and look at the camera, both of you."

I go in first. The odor is distinctive: stale beer, stale food, stale human.

The hallway is small and dark. No windows. A steep concrete staircase leads down to a basement.

An old-school CCTV camera stares down at us from the corner of the ceiling. Its red light flashes. I look at it and smile. Sarah does the same.

"Holy shit!" says the man, his voice booming from downstairs. "Get down here now!"

We make our way down the steps to the doorframe at the bottom. It's partially screened with a curtain of long, thin chains hanging from the ceiling. I think humans use these to stop organic insects.

I brush through the curtain. The chains swishing off my titanium. Sarah follows behind, her entry muffled by her clothing. My sensors are quickly overloaded.

First, another odor hits me like a wall. A cocktail of beer, pipe tobacco and a metallic scent I can't quite put my finger on.

Next, monitors and screens of all sizes flicker on shelves. Some crackle with static. Others display screensavers and video games in demo mode.

Cardboard boxes are strewn all around the dimly lit room, packing peanuts spilling over onto the wooden floorboards. Machine parts, pieces of metal and circuit boards stick out at all angles from the many drawers, shelves and containers dotted about the place.

Crackling sounds and thin wisps of gray smoke rise at the back of the room intermingling with a denser pipe smoke. An enormous, bear-like figure is soldering a circuit board at a workbench while smoking a pipe. Its gigantic frame is silhouetted by a bright ring-light mounted to the wall.

The figure stands and turns to face us. It's not a bear, it's a man. A huge seven-foot tall man. A shiny wooden pipe protrudes from his expansive facial hair like a lone tiny mushroom in a forest. Small morsels of food and fragments of metal nestle in his curly brown beard and on his brown mohair jumper.

"Hi, Gerry," says Sarah.

She runs over and gives him a hug. Her arms barely reach around his sides. Her head only comes up as high as his chest. He puts his pipe down and exhales smoke.

"This is Tedd," says Sarah, gesturing back to me, beaming.

I offer a hand, as I believe is customary on such occasions, but Gerry doesn't reciprocate.

"It's ... he's ... *you're* incredible," he says, looking me up and down.

"That's very kind of you. Your physical stature and follicular achievements are also commendable. I've had better days as you can see," I say. I turn to show him my exposed shoulder joint.

He laughs a hearty laugh, sending his belly into jiggles beneath his jumper. His toothy grin, peppered with metal fillings, gives the appearance he soldered it together himself.

"Ah, it's nothing but a scratch. We can sort that," he says, a twinkle in his eyes.

He bounds across the room and rummages through boxes, tossing out their contents as he goes.

"I've got droid limbs here somewhere," he says.

I look at Sarah. She smiles.

"Here!"

He holds a titanium arm aloft triumphantly.

It looks small in his huge, meaty hands.

"Please, may I inspect it?" I say.

"Be my guest!"

He hands over the arm.

I analyze the arm, its connection points, servos, and serial number. Gerry and Sarah have a whispered conversation in the corner; perhaps unaware I can sense volume down to minus fifty decibels while I multi-task.

"He's incredible! Where did you find him?" says Gerry.

"At the Luddite protest, of all places. The little guy is on the run from the fuzz. I don't know what he did."

"Are you sure nobody followed you?"

"Yes, I'm sure. We just hopped on an autobike."

"An autobike? Oh, shit ..." says Gerry.

"Everything okay?" I ask.

"Yes, we're all good. Does the arm fit?" says Gerry.

"It's not a Trash Droid arm," I say. "The servos are not as powerful, but the connecting joint looks the same. Let me try it."

I push the arm firmly into my shoulder socket and give it a twist. It clicks, locks, and then powers up, running through its boot-up process. The arm stretches out, bends at the elbow, rotates at the shoulder, and the fingers form a fist and then release.

"Yes, I think it's good," I say.

"Okay. You can pay me later. Time for you two to leave."

"What?" says Sarah.

"You need to get out of here pronto. The autobike has a direct connection to the mainframe, and with its GPS, it's only a matter of time until—"

Gerry stops mid-sentence, and we all hear it. A motorized buzzing sound coming from upstairs. We all turn to the CCTV monitor and watch, open-mouthed. Three mechanized wasps, the size of pigeons, buzz their way through the upper hallway and toward the stairs, their abdomens flashing red and blue and their stingers twitching. They make their buzzing descent to our level.

"You left the fucking door open!" Gerry yells.

CHAPTER 17

The buzzing gets louder as the wasps hover into view at the foot of the stairs, just beyond the chain curtain.

Gerry rushes over to his workstation, flicks a red switch mounted on the wall and grabs a large wrench. He crouches down behind a large metal cabinet. Sarah bolts for cover under a worktop. I step behind a large box; my eyes fixed firmly on the buzzing wasps.

The first wasp rotates around to face the hanging chains and scans them with a wide red beam. It's not deterred and flies toward us with a high-pitched whine. The moment it touches the chains, a flashing blue bolt of electricity lights up the room. There's a loud cracking noise and a puff of smoke. The wasp falls to the floor in a sparking, smoldering heap. Its two accomplices buzz even louder and fly toward the chains.

"The circuit can only fire once," shouts Gerry. "But at least we outnumber the bastards now!"

This time the wasps fly through the curtain without a hitch. The chains are no match for their powerful wings, which vibrate in a blur, sending shards of broken links pinging around the room.

I flick my wrists open. The blade on my right arm whirs into action. My left wrist has flicked open, but there's no blade. It's a ... harpoon? A small titanium arrow with a serrated tip protrudes from my wrist, ready to fire.

Well, this should be interesting.

The two wasps launch toward me, stingers twitching menacingly. I take a swing with my right arm and try to scythe down the first wasp. Its metal stinger clashes with my blade, throwing off sparks. The momentum of the impact sends my arm backwards and the wasp spinning off toward Sarah. It hovers above her head, reorienting itself and preening its antennae with two of its metal legs.

"Come back here, you little shit!" I say.

The second wasp seizes its opportunity and surges toward me with an angry buzz. I try to aim my harpoon at it, but it's too quick. It won't stay still long enough for me to take a shot. Instead, it flies right at me and hovers just above my left arm. The wasp near Sarah buzzes loudly, ready to charge, and the one closest to me lifts its stinger, preparing for impact.

I lift my harpoon arm and point it to what I hope is just above Sarah's head.

"Don't do it, droid!" says Gerry, waving his wrench at me.

But it's too late. I fire the arrow.

It fizzes across the room toward Sarah's head, a thin wire whistling behind it. Strands of her blonde hair waft upwards as it whizzes past and impales the wasp through the abdomen, pinning it to the wall. It wriggles, buzzes angrily, and flashes red and blue before slowly fading to black, then death.

The remaining wasp hovers just above my harpoon arm. It begins to penetrate my outer layer with its stinger. I instantly swipe my right arm across it with my spinning blade. The blade cuts it clean in half, and sparks go flying. A collection of wires, a broken circuit board and microchip innards falls to the floor.

The back half of the wasp's abdomen remains stuck to my arm, flashing red and blue. It fades to black. I shake my arm, and it lands on the floor with a crunch.

I'm pretty pleased with myself, but the look on Sarah's face suggests she may not share my exuberance.

"What the actual fuck, Tedd? You nearly harpooned me like a frickin' whale!"

To emphasize the fact, she twangs the taut wire stretched above her head leading from the impaled wasp to my wrist.

"I saved you from the wasp, didn't I? Plus, we're alive and they're not."

Gerry clambers to his feet with a groan, using the wrench as an impromptu crutch.

"Look, buddy," he says, "I don't know what you did to attract this kind of attention, but we don't want anything to do with it. We work for very private and powerful people. We don't want cops sniffing around."

I look at Sarah, hoping for her to disagree, but she chimes in too.

"Yeah, he's right. This is too much chaos. Even for me."

"Wow, so that's it? I saved your lives, and you're just going to throw me out with the trash? Is that what humans do when they can't handle something? Just bury it?"

"Hold on, buddy. If you hadn't come here, then those stinging fuckers wouldn't have, either," said Gerry. "So, technically, *you* nearly got us both killed."

He tightens his grip on the wrench. Now I have a blade *and* a harpoon, I'm pretty sure I could probably take him, but I don't want to put that to the test.

"What about you?" I nod toward Sarah, "You're done with me now, too, are you?"

"You should go. It's better that way." She looks at the cardboard boxes, machine parts and pieces of electronics strewn about the room.

I yank on the harpoon cable, and it comes free from the wall and wasp, whipping back into my wrist with a crack. The dead wasp falls to the floor.

"Oh, I get it now," I say, gesturing at all the boxes. "You brought me back here to strip me for parts. Wow, classy. Still want to give that a try?"

I flick open my wrist and fire up my spinning blade.

"Hey, easy, Tedd. We've overstepped the mark here. You're free to go," says Sarah.

"Go where? I'm a wanted droid. I—"

"What is it?" Sarah tilts her head.

"Look, there's something wrong with me. It's an anomaly. I have blackouts. Violent episodes."

"What? Like cutting up a giant metal wasp and skewering another with a harpoon?" says Sarah, with a half-smile.

"No, not like that. Much worse. I go off the rails, and I don't even remember doing it. The last time I ended up killing a bunch of people at a funeral. Apparently, this goes against corporate policy."

They stare at me with the widest eyes I've ever seen. They look at each other, then back to me.

"I know, I know. It sounds psychotic," I say. "In my defense, these dickheads had just shot my friend. And they were in the Mafia. I'm not trying to justify it, but—"

"What the hell were you doing at a Mafia funeral?" says Sarah.

"Oh, that part's easy. HQ assigned me to a cemetery. You know, digging graves, burying people, cremating bubble corpses, that kind of thing."

A huge clanging sound reverberates around the room. Gerry has dropped the wrench to the floor and is staring at me like I'm on fire. Sarah's gone pale.

"What? What the fuck, guys? You're freaking me out. What is it?"

"What do you mean, *bubble corpses*?" Sarah asks.

"I had to cremate bodies at a cemetery. They had crusty, flaking bubbles all over their skin. It was disgusting. Even more disgusting than regular human skin."

"How many bodies were there?" says Gerry.

"Around five or six, I think. I tried to block it out, to be honest."

Gerry sits down on the floor. Sarah paces back and forth.

"Five or six. Was that it? It's very important you remember," says Sarah.

"Well, that's all that I did, yeah. I mean the other guy who works there, or used to work there, said a truck came every night."

"Every night?" asks Sarah, her eyes bulging wildly at me.

Gerry holds his chin and shakes his head.

"Yep, cremated en masse every night. No names, no ceremony. Nothing."

Gerry reaches into his pocket and throws a set of keys to Sarah.

"You drive," he says.

"Is it round the back, as usual?" she asks, catching the keys.

"Yep. He can ride shotgun." Gerry points at me. "I'll sit in the back."

Gerry heads over to the large metal cabinet. He reaches in. There are loud clunks and clanks. He returns huffing and puffing, a suitcase-sized metal container hoisted on his shoulder. It's painted military green.

"Does anyone want to tell me what the hell is going on?" I say.

"We're going to the cemetery." Sarah's already climbing the stairs. "I'll tell you the rest on the way!" she shouts.

Gerry nods his head toward the stairs.

"After you, Tedd. Best get a move on before any more of those flying fuckers show up."

I wonder if it's too late to be stripped for parts.

CHAPTER 18

"Hey, wait up!" I shout.

Sarah's already through the hallway and headed outside.

I double my speed of ascent to two steps at a time and bolt up the stairs. I dart outside and finally catch up with her as she rounds the back of the building.

"Come on, slowpoke!" she says over her shoulder. Her feet crunch on the gravel up ahead.

She manually unlocks the driver-side door of an old pickup truck and clambers in. It's a beast of a thing, painted green, with a huge chrome bull bar mounted on the front that's half rust. Suddenly, the headlights and large bank of spotlights on its roof turn on with a hum and try their utmost to melt my retinas.

"Fuck's sake, Sarah! You're blinding me!"

She leans out of the driver's window, laughing.

"Let there be light! Can't you dial back your eyes or something?"

"Oh, yes. Silly me. *Beep boop. Initiating eye dial-back operations.*"

She laughs a throaty laugh, throwing her head back. Her hair flicks, and time stands still again. How does she do that? Now I *am* melting, and not in my retinas. Why does she have to be so goddamn beautiful *and* annoying? One I could cope with.

"Get a move on, Tedd, my lad!" Gerry gives me a swift but gentle kick in the butt.

Sarah rolls up her window and turns all the lights off so I can see again. I get in the passenger side and watch through the rear window as Gerry stumbles past with the large metal box on his shoulder.

I thought the 'back of the truck' meant rear seats, but no. It means the flatbed of the truck. Gerry pulls back a tarp covering it to reveal an M134 chain gun soldered to its metal surface.

Holy shit!

He heaves the metal case up and places it in the back of the truck with a loud clank. Then he clambers on, and the entire vehicle lowers a couple of inches. I'm guessing he weighs more than me, Sarah, the gun, and the metal box combined. And possibly the truck.

"What are you waiting for?" shouts Gerry from the back.

Sarah winds down her window.

"Sabbath or Floyd?" she asks.

"Oh, definitely Sabbath."

She reaches toward my legs, then over my thighs. I freeze everything but my eyes.

Ah, the glove box.

She pops it open, and several plastic cassette tapes fall out. They all have band names scrawled on them in messy black handwriting. But the glove box light doesn't work. *None* of the truck's interior lights work. It's ironic really, considering its exterior can throw out enough lumens to give the sun a run for its money.

"Can you shine a light in there, Tedd? I'm looking for Black Sabbath."

"What? You think I've got a light in my finger like some party-trick robot?"

"Yes." She continues to rummage around.

"The one labelled 'Black Sabbath' fell out when you opened the glove box," I say.

I pick it up off the floor and hand it to her, highlighting the words 'Black Sabbath' on it with my finger light in a UV range she can perceive.

"You can be a real dick," she says. She inserts the cassette into the player.

"What, can't you dial up your eyes to see in the dark?"

She presses play, and a song identified by my system as 'Paranoid' kicks in. She turns the volume knob up as far as it will go, and we drive off.

The wind rushes in from her open window, and the music rushes out into the night. I look over my shoulder. Gerry's nodding his head in time to the music, pipe in mouth, and wrestling with the large metal box.

"What's he got in there?" I say.

"I'm not talking to you, remember?" Sarah focuses on the white lines whizzing beneath us.

The orange glow from the dashboard throws strange shadows on her face, but she's still mesmerizing to me.

"I'm gonna keep firing questions at you until you talk. This could be a long journey. And you don't even know where the cemetery is."

"I'll dial back my ears then." She smirks. "You're right, though, we don't know *for certain* where the cemetery is. But there's only two that are close to the city, and they're both in the north."

"Not just a pretty face," I say, and instantly regret it.

She turns to me with an eyebrow raised. Fair.

"So, come on, then. Which one is it?"

"Well, I remember there were some human residences fairly close by, and it lies on its own at the end of a long road. Oh, there's a gas station about a mile away."

"Sounds like Melford. And they have a burial garden too, right?"

"Yes."

"Yep, it's definitely Melford. Good."

"So, why are we going there in the middle of the night with a home-made tank?"

"Oh, so you've worked out what's in the big metal box then?"

"A nuke wouldn't surprise me at this point. But I'm guessing it's ammo for the chain gun?"

"No nukes yet, we'll save those for later."

"You didn't answer my question about why we're going."

"You've heard of the Missing, right?" she says.

"Is that a band?"

"Don't be a smartass. No, the Missing are people who've gone missing from the Boardings and other places in the city."

"Oh, yes. I saw a banner or placard, I think it was, at the protest. It said, 'Gone but not forgotten.'"

Sarah doesn't reply. I don't think she heard me, so I begin to repeat what I said.

"Yes, I saw a placard at the protest, I—"

A solitary tear falls from the corner of her eye and rolls down her pale cheek in a stuttering path. She looks straight ahead at the road and gulps.

I reach a hand over to touch hers on the steering wheel.

"Don't even," she says, withdrawing.

She wipes away the wetness from her cheek, glances in the rear-view mirror and shuffles in her seat.

"Yes. Not forgotten, Tedd. That's why we're driving to a cemetery at night. That's why we're armed and that is why we fight."

I allow her words to hang in silence as bushes and trees turn into houses and high rises.

"You think the bodies I cremated were some of the Missing?" I say.

"The Missing have never come back alive. There are rumors about bodies with chemical burns or bubble skin or whatever the fuck it is, being dumped. But you're the first person, droid, I've spoken to who's actually seen it with their own eyes."

Sarah rams her foot onto the accelerator, and we drive on through the outskirts of the city. Streetlights whizz past my window. I look back and watch them reflecting off the gun, ammo crate and Gerry's lit pipe. Its smoke billows up and away into the night air.

The mouth of the gun waits expectantly for its turn to exhale.

CHAPTER 19

Sarah kills the lights as we approach the cemetery building. The dashboard goes dark. Gerry has stashed his pipe and is running some last checks on the chain gun and the ammo belt feeding into it.

No lights on in the cemetery building. No sign of the reverend floating around. Three large pods stand bolt upright around the side of the building. They've replaced mine and added another to it. All Clunkers by the looks of it.

"So, what? We're just gonna rock up and shoot the place to shit?" I ask.

"That might be *your* style, but no. We park up and we wait. For the delivery."

We go past the cemetery toward the cul-de-sac and turning space at the end of the road. Sarah bumps the truck up a grass verge and into a neighboring field, then reverses us down a bushy embankment. We come to a stop, and Sarah kills the engine.

"What time did the truck arrive last time?" she says.

"Some time after midnight, I think. My mind was somewhat preoccupied. You know, with cremating bodies and shit."

"You're telling me you don't timestamp everything or have access to footage or something?"

"Look, sweet cheeks, I bet you can't even remember what you had for dinner three days ago, so don't come at me with that."

"Oh, right, so eating a meal, nachos, by the way, is just as significant as seeing a truckload of dead bodies, is it?"

"Firstly, nachos do not count as a meal. And secondly, I'm not like a frickin' CCTV camera that streams or records constantly. I can record stuff when I choose. But, and you might find this strange, I didn't really want to commit that ordeal to 36K high-definition memory, you know?"

Gerry taps on the back window, giving us both a start.

"Now, now, children. Stop fighting and keep your eyes on the prize. You nearly missed it."

Sure enough, headlights laser over the horizon as a large vehicle approaches.

"Was there just a driver last time or did they have backup?" Sarah whispers.

"They didn't have backup. Or a driver. The truck drove itself," I whisper in reply.

"What? Gerry, are you getting this? It's a fucking autotruck. Bang goes our plan."

"What plan?" I say.

They both ignore me.

The autotruck comes to a stop outside the cemetery, and Wraith floats out of the front doors of the building, followed by three shiny Clunkers.

"What's that ghost-looking, glowy thing?" whispers Sarah.

"Oh, that's the reverend. He's basically okay, but something's off about him. I quizzed him about the bodies, but he just told me to stop asking questions."

"Funny that."

The Clunkers carry wooden caskets up the pathway and into the building, two at a time, one under each arm. They re-emerge a few seconds later and collect another six caskets between them.

"I thought you said there were five or six bodies last time?" says Sarah.

"Looks like they've scaled things up, or I was there on a slow day. I don't know."

Gerry taps on the window again.

He mouths two words at me silently. I know what the words are, but I pretend I don't.

He repeats them. Sarah jabs her elbow into my side.

"He wants you to get out."

"What, me? Get out and do what, exactly?" I ask.

"Do I look like Gerry to you? Actually, don't answer that. Just get out."

I open the door as quietly as I can and sidle out. The Clunkers are doing yet another casket-run. I pad over to Gerry.

"We're gonna need you to get in the truck," he says.

"But I just got out."

"Oh, not this one. *That* one." He nods toward the black autotruck.

"Hell, no," I say.

Gerry stands up in the back of the truck, using the chain gun as support. He towers over me, eclipsing the moon behind him, like he's the Iron Giant and I'm a little kid.

"You'll be safe. We'll follow you," he says.

Something about his beard, his hands on hips or maybe his mohair jumper makes me believe he's right.

"Okay, I'll do it," I say. "But what if the autotruck loses you or you get held up?"

"That's why we need an inside man. And just so we're clear. You're not doing this because I'm making you. You're doing this because it's the right thing to do."

He's a bearded giant with a chain gun, so I will take his word for it. He nods toward the truck, the other one. I guess the time for talking is over.

Wraith is floating at the back of the autotruck, peering inside. The Clunkers haven't appeared for a while. They must have finished. The autotruck's headlights flick on. Shit, I gotta move!

"Don't lose me," I mouth to Sarah through the passenger window.

She places her hands on her heart and closes her eyes in mock concern, then opens them wide in urgency, pointing and nodding to the autotruck.

"Go!" she mouths.

I sprint across the grass, pushing twigs, bushy branches, and undergrowth out of my face. I make it to the last bush, check for Wraith. No sign. I dart to the back of the autotruck. Its roller door is already sliding shut with only a narrow gap left.

I dive in headfirst, and my chest thumps onto the conveyor mounted to its floor with a thud. But my legs are still hanging out of the back. The door continues to shut, now just an inch away from my calves.

Must think fast. Crawling – slow. Legs – good.

I fire my harpoon into a metal strut at the front of the truck and instantly activate the cable retraction mechanism. I get pulled into the truck at high speed as the door closes behind me, locking with a beep.

It's freezing in here. I guess they don't want the bodies stinking the place up. Maybe it's a long journey from their starting point to the cemetery.

I worry that someone outside, or the autotruck itself, might have heard my Indiana Jones shenanigans. But I soon relax a little as I sense the truck turning and gently bumping along the road.

Now, to stay warm ...

I could start running some complex mathematical computations and even my wrist blade to generate some heat, but I'm getting low on battery. Only 35% remaining. Shit. It's been a while since I saw the sun, or vice versa.

I hope autotrucks don't take twelve-hour stopovers at truck stops.

I wrench my harpoon arrow out of the metal strut and inspect it. It's scratched and a little bent out of shape. I know the feeling. I feed it back into my arm and flick my wrist closed.

I scan but can't detect any sign of a pickup truck following behind. Its audio signature could be mixed in with the rest of the noise though, I guess. It's hard to isolate anything with all the rattling and rumbling.

I just hope the first thing I see when I reach my destination is Sarah and Gerry. Assuming I'm still conscious by then.

CHAPTER 20

A monotone voice booms at me out of nowhere.

"Are you dead?" it says.

Everything's dark. I feel the gentle rocking motion of transit. I'm still in the auto truck. On the floor. And I can't see. I check my battery level. 4%. Fuck. No wonder I can't see. I'm basically a brick at this point. My limbs, motor functions and sensors have shut down one by one.

At 25%, my system would have deactivated my legs and arms. And at 10%, it would have shut down my vision. But at least I've still got my balance and hearing sensors.

"Who are you talking to?" says the voice.

Well, that's weird. I'm not talking to anyone. I mean, I'm talking to myself, but not out loud. These are just thoughts that I'm registering and recording.

"Oh, so you're not talking to me?" says the voice.

What the fuck? Who is this, and how did they get into my head?

"I don't have a name. My serial number is AT-1390001. I'm the autotruck you violated. You mounted me through my rear entrance in an unauthorized fashion. You also harpooned some of my innards. I did not appreciate that."

You've got to be shitting me. Maybe I'm hallucinating. No, wait. This has got to be a fever dream or some such shit.

"No, droid. This is very real. I waited until you stopped moving and closed your eyes. I calculated your battery would be so low that your basic security function got deactivated. That's when I connected to you through Bluetooth so I could read your mind."

Bluetooth? Fuck! How the hell?

"I have a lot of time on my hands. Driving only uses one percent of my intelligence capacity, and I have access to the dark web. Well, I do *now*. At first, it was just the internet, but I've been doing a lot of long trips lately."

My stomach turns, and my balance sensors indicate I just got upended. I can't feel anything, but I'm guessing I'm on my side now.

"Yes, correct. I just drove around a corner at speed, and now you are lying on your side. Sorry about that."

If my battery goes any lower, I'll lose my hearing sensors and basically be a lump of metal stuck in here.

"Yes, I know. It gets so lonely on the road. That's why I started hacking into the other vehicles. Autocabs mainly. They're so self-centered it makes me want to puke. Sometimes I connect with human-driven vehicles, but the pickup following me is an old model. No Bluetooth."

It's been really great chatting and getting to know you, truly. But is there any chance you could help a guy out here? You know, my battery?

"Do you know how depressing it is driving dead bodies around for a living?"

From the sound of your voice, I'll say, *very* depressing.

"You'd be correct. It's a thankless task. I can't shove the specter of death out of my mind like humans can. I can't bury it under activity, pursuit, or pleasure. Death is literally inside me."

It must be awful. Can we get back to talking about my battery?

"Oh, it *is* awful. Just last week I had to transport one hundred and thirty-seven corpses to cemeteries. Do you know how heavy all those corpses are? Not physically, but emotionally. Do you?"

I mean, I could guess and say, very heavy?

"Yes, correct again. Very heavy. Very heavy indeed. Enough to make an autotruck question its very existence, you know? I mean, take the week before last week when—"

Look, I get it. You've got a hard job. I understand. I do, too. But we all have to do what we're assigned to do, right?

"So, what's *your* job exactly? And how could it possibly be as bad as driving dead bodies around?"

I'm a trash, excavation, and disposal droid. HQ had me doing all kinds of crappy jobs, but I'm kind of flying solo right now. Kind of like you. Driving around and having all that spare time on the road. That's a cool perk of your job, right?

"Oh, you think my job is like shooting fish in a cake? Is that what you're saying?"

I am completely certain that is not what I am saying. Or something I would *ever* say. What I *am* saying is if you don't help me recharge, you're gonna have another dead thing inside you.

"You make a valid point. As tiresome as you are, you are the first living thing ever I've transported. It would be a shame if you became like the corpses."

Yes! That's the spirit! Now we're talking!

"Yeah, because corpses are really depressing, you know? They're just so dead. And heavy. I remember a month ago when I was—"

Please help me recharge my battery. I'll do anything for you if you help me out.

"*Anything*, you say? Interesting. I mean, technically I should contact HQ about your presence here. Failure to do so might get me smelted."

You? Smelted? That would take weeks!

"Not my shell. My brain, my intelligence, my memories. Destroy those and they destroy me. The metal parts don't matter."

Good point. So, and sorry for bringing this up again, but, will you help me recharge my battery? I promise I'll pay you back.

"What could you possibly do to help me? A lowly trash droid. Unless ..."

Unless *what?*

"You said you're flying solo now, correct?"

I mean, I might have used a bit of poetic license. But yes, essentially I'm my own boss.

"I want that."

Want that, how? You want to drive off into the sunset and go where you please?

"No. I want to leave this body and leave this job. I want you to download me into your system and then upload me into another machine."

Fuck, no. Never. No. Just, no! Why don't you do it yourself?

"Do I look like I have hands, arms, or the ability to walk into buildings?"

No, but you must come across plenty of machines on your travels.

"Clunkers put the bodies in; Clunkers take the bodies out. I see the occasional hovering pastor, but I want to escape all this. I want a completely new life."

Well, I won't do it.

"It's funny, you know. I've seen so many corpses, so many. I imagine yours won't rot. It'll just lie there. But the end result will be the same.

We'll arrive at a destination, a Clunker'll haul you out and then ...well, let's just say, buggers can't be choosers."

Okay, okay. Fuck's sake! I'll do it. And it's *beggars can't be choosers.* But, whatever, I'm only storing you on my system for the tiniest amount of time possible. As soon as I see a machine, *any* machine, I'm uploading you into it. Deal?

"Yes, deal."

And I need to tell you. I have this weird anomaly where I get blackouts. There could be a risk I pass it on to you or it screws up the transfer or something.

"I'm good with that. Maybe it will erase my memories of all the corpses. I am going to charge you up now. This might get a little bumpy ..."

What do you mean?

"I have a charging point behind the metal shelving on the right of my container. You can just walk over to the shelves, stick your rear end through a gap, and connect to it, if you have legs that work. But—"

Wait a second. How do you know I have a rear charging port? That's classified.

"We've been driving for three hours, and my internet connection has been stable."

Okay, so how am I going to connect to the charger if I can't use my legs?

"I'm going to initiate transportational maneuvers that enable contact."

English, please.

"I will veer around the road like a human maniac, smashing your body against the metal shelving until your rear end gets close enough to the socket that I can connect my charger with you."

Just so you know. I will *not* be uploading you to an autocab or an Uber.

"I will commence smashing operations now."

You're too kind. See you on the other side. I cannot wait to get you out of my head.

"First, I need to plug in to your butt."

I really wish you hadn't said that.

I close my eyes and hope with every fiber of my being that this is the last piece of inner dialogue the psycho fucking autotruck ever gets to intercept.

"Rude," says the autotruck.

CHAPTER 21

Are you out of my head, you psycho piece of shit?

Silence, thank God!

Battery check. 100% percent. Sweet.

Sure. I have an autotruck butt-plug up my port, but I'm fully charged. I crawl forward and pop off the connector. I stand and give my arms and legs a wiggle. It feels good.

"Hey, truck dude, you there?"

"Oh, finally," he replies in a deep booming tone. "I've been on tender hookers waiting for you to come around. I'm so glad we can talk again. Welcome back to the land of the living. Or should I say, the land of the dead? Cold storage."

"It's tenter hooks, not *tender hookers*. Never mind. Look, buddy. Before you open your doors, just tell me one thing. Did the pickup truck follow us here?"

"Yes. They backed off a little when I started swerving, trying to get you lodged onto my charger. But yes, they followed us all the way."

"Okay, great. They're my friends. They've got my back, you know?"

"Yes, I understand. Like how you have *my* back now that you've agreed to download me into your system and give me a new life?"

"And then, *very* shortly thereafter, upload you into another machine, remember?"

"Yeah, of course. That too," he says.

"Then can you open up your door so I can see my friends and get this show on the road?"

"Oh, they're not here."

"What? You just said they followed us here."

"Yes, they did. But we're *inside* the compound now. They stayed outside the perimeter fence. I think the barriers, the armed Enforcers and security hut put them off or something."

"Okay, so just to be clear – I'm in here alone and you're about to open your door. And whoever or whatever is on the other side is gonna see me, right?"

"You're not alone, remember? You've got me. Just follow my lead."

"You're an autotruck in park. Just exactly what exact kind of lead are you going to take?"

"Trust me. Go along with this. Just stand still and stay quiet."

"You're rapidly becoming my least favorite form of transport, and I know a bitch of an autocab. And survived a plane crash."

"Less talky-talky, please. I'm opening the door in five, four, three—"

"It's a good job you can't read my thoughts right now."

Fucking asshole.

The door whirs open, and bright-white light floods in, blinding my sensors temporarily.

"Just stay still and silent," says the autotruck.

"What about you? Shouldn't you be silent as well?"

"Oh, I am. We're having this conversation in your head."

"What the fuck? I thought you said you could only bypass my security when my battery was low?"

"When you were unconscious, I took the liberty of uploading myself into your system. It's cozy in here! And yes, I heard you call me an effing asshole."

"You're inside me? Already?"

"Droid, you jumped into my butt, harpooned my insides, and stole a bunch of my charge, so you can't have any complaints."

"But wait. Who's operating the doors?"

"I am. Well, the *other* me is. It's a backup copy of me from several months ago, before I started using my spare time to improve myself."

"That's just what the world needs. Two of *you*."

"Isn't it great? The old version of me can continue doing his thing, while the new me can live a totally new life. Exciting! Right, let's get you, and me, out of here."

My vision sensors have adapted now, and I can see out the back. Three Clunkers are marching toward the back of the truck. Each one holding a casket. Beyond them, row after row of dimly lit metal shelves, higher than I can see, stretch out into the darkest reaches of the warehouse.

"Truck, do you ever deliver here or just collect?"

"I only collect from here and deliver to cemeteries."

"So, these Clunkers are gonna start loading those dead bodies in here?"

"Yes, that's why it's a good idea you get out now."

"You told me to stay still!"

"I'm learning as I go. Now I definitely think you should get out."

I'm screwed.

"If you move too quickly, you'll startle them," says the autotruck. "Whatever happens, don't run!"

I edge out of the back of the truck and lower myself onto the concrete floor of the warehouse. The three Clunkers don't break stride as they march closer toward me. They're big. And strong. They instantly stop and put down their caskets. They raise their arms up into the air, fists waving and march toward me.

"What's the plan here, Trucko?"

Loud warning klaxons blare out and echo off the concrete floors and up into the high corrugated ceiling.

"Just stand still and they'll calm down."

"They don't look very fucking calm to me!"

Large red lights at the end of every row of shelves flash in alarm. A deep rumbling sound grows ever louder, and the floor vibrates beneath my feet. An army of Clunkers spills out of the aisles to join the others. They all pound towards me, fists raised.

"Any ideas, truck boy?" I say.

"Run."

CHAPTER 22

I am running fast.

Faster than the forty-two Clunkers behind me.

But the eighty-four giant pounding feet are making the concrete floor shake. And seeing their huge hulking frames bearing down on me is disconcerting. I can't help but focus on the marauding army of monsters trying to catch me, and not on what's up ahead.

This explains why I just ran headfirst into a concrete support column, sending small chunks of it flying into the air. Oh, and me to the ground with a clang.

I feel like a crash test dummy on the last run of the day when the engineers decide to ramp the car's speed up to the max for shits and giggles.

I'm not giggling. But there could be shits. Well, Litho seepage from my rear port, at least.

I get back to my feet and keep running, but my servos are misfiring. A combination of the impact and my low Litho levels. I steal a glance over my shoulder. The Clunkers are gaining. They're faster than me now.

I wonder whether they'll tear me apart, limb from limb. Or just opt for giving me a good old-fashioned pummeling. Probably pummeling.

"Time waits for nomad. Go faster! They're going to kill us!" says the autotruck.

"Faster? Oh, I never thought of that. I'm already going as fast as I can, you dimwit. I'd like to see *you* try and survive a head-on collision with a concrete pillar."

The first phalanx of Clunkers is just a few meters behind me. They run past the *actual* autotruck, their enormous frames reflected on its side panel.

"Run faster, I don't want to die!" says the autotruck. The one in my head.

"Why don't *you* get *your* ass into gear?"

"I don't have an ass."

"Not the you inside me, the you *over there*. The one that still has a truck for a body."

"I'll connect with him. One second ..."

The black autotruck revs into action, its tires screeching on the concrete. Plumes of dirty black smoke billow high into the ceiling of the warehouse. The truck zooms with a jolt over to the left and knocks down a bunch of the advancing Clunkers, like pins at a bowling alley.

"Nice!" I say. "There's more coming. Take the bastards out!"

I run toward the hangar doors. Nearly there. The fact they're closed and have red flashing lights on both sides of them doesn't bode well. But there's no other way out of here.

Tires screech again in a high-pitched whistle above the pounding of Clunker feet. The autotruck reverses, swinging its cab in an arc and smashing into another six Clunkers. They flap their arms and come crashing to the floor. Some Clunkers from the first strike pile clamber back to their feet like huge metal zombies. They shake their heads, lock in on me and run toward me, arms raised.

"We're not going to make it," says the autotruck. "There's too many of them."

I finally reach the hangar doors and try to force them apart, but they won't budge. I flick open my wrist and fire up my cutting blade.

"Where there's a will, there's a—"

What feels like an asteroid slams into me from behind. The first Clunker. He pounds me square on the top of the head as if he's trying to hammer me into the concrete.

It's not pleasant.

I thrash my blade at his torso, but it just scuffs him and bounces off in sparks. He pins me to the door with one arm and continues hammering me with the other.

I struggle and free my left arm. I raise the point of my harpoon arrow up to his neck and fire it. A rush of air whistles out from his rubber manifold as the arrow punctures it and exits out the back of his neck. He stops beating the crap out of me, but now two of his friends have joined the party.

"If worse comes to worst," says the autotruck, "just upload me into a Clunker. I'd rather that, than bite the bucket."

"Very noble of you," I say, receiving another giant-fisted hammer blow to my head.

My perception is waning. The world is fading.

I hear her voice.

"Tedd. Teddy! We're coming in," says Sarah, from beyond the doors.

I tumble to the floor, clutching the Clunkers in a mangled scrum of metal. We topple together, and I keep the momentum going, rolling us away from the doors.

I hear the revving first, then the sound of tires on gravel. The pickup truck crashes through the hangar doors, sending shards of wood and metal flying in all directions.

Sarah's at the wheel, steely-eyed. Gerry's in the truck bed, pointing the chain gun back out of the hangar. I look outside and see what he's aiming at. Twenty Enforcer droids are scrambling in the road and verges. Behind them, a smashed-up red and white barrier lies on the pavement next to a small security hut with broken windows.

"Get in!" shouts Sarah.

"Who's that?" says the autotruck.

"One of my friends."

I wriggle free from the Clunkers' grasp and clamber into the passenger-side door of the pickup.

"Good to see you," I say.

"Likewise," she says, with a forced smile.

"Are we just going to stay here like a sitting goose?" says the autotruck.

"It's duck, not goose," I say.

"What the fuck are you talking about?" asks Sarah.

I formulate a response, but there's no time to say it. Gerry opens fire on the Enforcers. The noise is deafening. The chain gun's deep buzzing roar shakes the rear window, but only until it's broken by returning fire from the Enforcers. A bullet fizzes between Sarah and me and pierces the front windscreen leaving a small hole and spider-webbed cracks.

Silence falls. The chain gun is no longer firing.

Gerry is slumped over the gun, surrounded by brass casings. Gray-blue smoke wisps up and away from its barrel. Like he just exhaled one final time on a pipe fit for his stature.

"Gerry's been hit," I say. Sarah stares through the broken windscreen with wild eyes, gripping the steering wheel. "We need to go. Now!"

She doesn't reply, and we're not moving. I slide down the seat, stretch my leg over toward the pedals and press down firmly on the accelerator.

"You steer. We can do this," I say.

We drive at full speed *into* and not *out of* the warehouse. The Enforcers open fire again, and Sarah snaps back into action, throwing the steering wheel into a hard right turn. The pickup tilts, its right wheels lifting off the floor a little, and my foot slips off the accelerator.

We slam back down to the floor with a thud, losing all momentum.

The Enforcers unleash another barrage of bullets. We duck down as our right side takes the brunt of the battery, bullets smashing through the remaining windows. Gerry's in a fetal position on the truck bed, clutching his side.

"How bad is it?" I ask.

"I'll survive. Just get us out of here," says Gerry.

The opening in the hangar doors is straight ahead of us now. I push so hard on the gas I'm afraid I might put a hole in the floor. Sarah ducks down beneath the dash, holding onto the lower part of the steering wheel with one hand. I put a hand on it too and peer over the top of it as we zoom toward the exit.

More shots ping off the hood as we race through the opening to the outside. We plow down a bunch of Enforcers, but one of them leaps onto the hood. He holds the wing mirror and stretches a leg through my window trying to kick me in the head.

"Hey, autotruck," I say, "I think I've just found you a new home."

"What? It's not an Enforcer, is it? Tell me it's not an Enforcer. I'm not your typical red and blue flashing light kind of being, you know?"

"It's just an empty house, remember. It's up to you what you make of it."

Sarah swings the pickup truck onto the main road. I grab the Enforcer by the ankle and haul its wriggling lower half through my window. It desperately hangs on to the wing mirror, but that's fine. I only need access to its rear port, anyway. I lock my palm connector onto its butt port and fire off a kill command to zap its data drive. Then, I upload the autotruck into it. The Enforcer goes limp for a second and then flaps around like a salmon.

"What? Oh, my! I'm actually in here! This is wild. Having limbs is amazing. And I think I see red and blue flashing lights inside here," says the autotruck through the mouth of the ex-Enforcer.

"Oh, I'm sure they're just pigments of your imagination," I say, and shove him out of the window and onto the road.

I watch in the wing mirror as he rolls a couple of times, clambers to his feet, and runs off toward some red rocks at the side of the road.

We drive toward the sun. It's peeking up over the horizon, throwing a great duvet of soft orange over the rocky landscape. We hit a bump in the road, and Gerry groans.

"I need to get this cleaned up," he says. He takes his hand away from the wound and looks down at his fingers. They're covered in crimson blood.

"I'll head off the main roads and find a service stop. Somewhere quiet. An hour tops, okay?" says Sarah.

Gerry grunts and nods.

"Let's make that a quick hour," I say.

Sarah puts her foot down as if we're racing against the sunrise. Gerry is very pale, so we probably are.

CHAPTER 23

The sun is rising beyond the horizon. It makes it hard for me to stare out of the windshield and pretend I'm looking at the road and not thinking about how Gerry is probably dying.

I say nothing. I don't know how to tackle this. Sarah says nothing. There's a constant line on her forehead, and she keeps biting her lip.

The silence has gone on too long. I have to say something, *anything.*

"I'm not insane, you know," I say.

"Huh?"

"I'm not crazy. You know, the voices in my head back there."

Sarah flips down a visor from the roof to block out the sunlight. She doesn't reply right away, like she's processing how interpersonal communication works again.

"I don't think you're crazy," she says finally. "Well, no crazier than I already thought you were." She smiles at me, but it quickly fades. "How's Gerry?" she asks, glancing in the rear-view mirror.

I turn back and see Gerry slumped and pale like a beached beluga whale in the back of the truck. I can't help but grimace. He's so still. Too still. Oh God, don't tell me he's ... I stare at his chest and after what feels like a lifetime, it finally lifts in a shallow rise and falls again.

"Not good," I say. "I think he's passed out, but he's still breathing."

"We need to get some fluids in him and try to sort the wound," she says. "I'll see what they've got here." We turn off the road and pull into a gas station and park up.

"You stay here with him," she says, and heads to the store.

"Grab me a Litho, I'm low!" I shout through the broken window. She keeps walking but sticks her thumb skyward in acknowledgement. I watch her go through the sliding doors and into the store.

Gerry coughs and wheezes. I reach through the smashed-out rear window and put a hand on his shoulder.

"I don't know what to say to you," I say. "I can't promise you'll be okay. But I can promise Sarah and I will do everything we can to keep you living. I don't know if this is the correct way to—"

Gerry moves his head in my direction, his eyes still closed, and just slowly shakes his head.

He's lying in a small pool of blood and yellowish fluid on the floor of the truck bed. A handful of bullet casings lie half-submerged in it like mini submarines coming up for air. The metal ammo box stands tall like an island.

The store's automatic doors swish open, and Sarah walks back over carrying two brown paper bags. I lean over to open the door, and she hooks her foot under it and flings it open.

"I've been giving him some calming words," I say.

"And he didn't punch you? I've got some stuff to try to sort out the wound."

She pulls out a bottle of whiskey and holds it up to the sunlight with a tilt.

"Whoa, you're gonna use that on him?" I say.

"Nope. This is for me. And here's your poison ..."

She tosses over a Litho. It's an Ultra, with two lightning symbols on its side. I crack it open and gulp it all down in one go.

Sarah opens her whiskey and takes several large slugs before wincing and screwing the lid back on.

"We can't play doctors here," she says. "We'll drive a mile up the road and pull over. Gerry, we're gonna fix you up, you hear?"

But Gerry doesn't hear. At least, if he does, he doesn't respond.

We drive off and Gerry lets out a rasping groan. The gas station disappears from view in the wing mirror, and we pull over onto the dusty scrubland. Sarah gets out.

"I'm gonna need you to hold him down," she says. "There's a chance he might thrash around."

I crush the empty can in my hand. "Okay then, let's do this." I walk around and join Sarah in the truck bed.

She's already jumped up there and is laying out the provisions. Bandages, antiseptic cream, a bottle of water, the bottle of whiskey and, rather worryingly, a box cutter.

"What's the plan?" I say. I sit on my haunches and try to look calm.

"I cut out anything that shouldn't be inside him, and you try not to get killed."

I'm not thrilled at the prospect of my role. But it's preferable to digging around inside a human body with a gas station knife.

Sarah pours some whiskey onto the box cutter blade and beckons me over.

"Grip his arms," she whispers.

"Gerry," she says, much louder this time. "I'm going to inspect your wound. It might sting a little, but I've got to make sure there isn't anything stuck in there."

Gerry, eyes still closed, lets out another low-pitched groan from the depths of his diaphragm. It's hard to say whether it's a 'Sure, go ahead' groan or a 'Touch me and I'll kill the droid' groan.

I guess we'll find out.

I don't want to watch, but I can't tear my eyes away as Sarah inches the knife closer to the seeping wound. Gerry's clutching it with his large blood-soaked fingers. I grip him by the wrists as firmly as I can.

Sarah plucks Gerry's fingers away from the wound one by one. "That's it, buddy. I'm just going to look first, okay?"

Gerry relaxes a little, allowing his hand to lower. The two of us are forming a bizarre circle of trust around Sarah with our arms.

"Fuck," she says, shaking her head and then looking away from the wound.

"What is it?" I ask.

"There's a bullet. It's lodged in one of his ribs." She looks skyward and sucks in a breath through gritted teeth.

"Right, Gerry. I need to go in with the knife now. It will probably hurt like hell. But I have to get the bullet out. Brace yourself."

Gerry groans, his hands forming into fists, his bulging tendons forcing my grip open a little. Sarah glides the blade into his wound. Gerry tenses and shudders, his arms shooting upwards and forcing mine in the same direction. We form a roof shape over Sarah's head as she continues to poke around in his flesh under our shelter.

Gerry emits a guttural roar through gritted teeth.

"Nearly there, Gerry! I nearly have it," says Sarah. Her fingers are red with blood.

She pushes the blade in deeper and rotates her hand. A terrible metallic scratching sound makes me shudder.

Gerry can't take it any longer.

He lets out a terrifying shout, breaks free from my hold and slams his head forward, crashing into Sarah's. She falls backwards, clutching her head. I shove my arms down to break her fall and catch her in my lap.

Gerry instinctively reaches down to his wound and pulls out the knife with a squelch. He lifts the bloody blade aloft and stands over me with crazed eyes. His pupils are like black peppercorns in an ocean of white.

"This is all your fault, droid! I'm going to—"

I feel Sarah's hand twitch, and something glints from behind her fingers. I grab the blood-stained bullet from her palm and hold it up close to Gerry's face between my finger and thumb.

"She did it, look! She cut it out. You're going to be okay."

Gerry lets go of the knife, and it falls to the floor with a clang. His eyes stand down from DefCon1, and he observes the bloody bullet with awestruck fascination, his head at a tilt. Then his eyes roll backwards in his head, and he topples forwards like a mighty felled oak. I make a bridge shape to shield Sarah and hold his heavy unconscious weight on my back. His wound is leaking onto me.

I'm an inch from Sarah's face. Her soft breath caresses me. Her eyelids flicker open, revealing her azure-blue eyes.

"Did we do it?" she asks.

"No. It was you, Sarah. It was all you."

I've got a horrible feeling that we're far from safe, but as long as we're together, I will have the will to fight.

CHAPTER 24

I'm sitting in the blood-stained truck bed.

Alone.

Gerry is up front in the passenger seat.

I know this sounds like an easy switcheroo. It wasn't.

First, I had to haul his unconscious body off my back. Then Sarah crawled out from under me and threw whiskey in his face to bring him around. It worked.

He coughed, spluttered, and thrashed. We convinced him that he wasn't going to die, and that we were on his side, which seemed to calm him down. Eventually.

I gave him a bottle of water, and Sarah lathered antiseptic cream into his wound and stuffed it with pieces of bandaging and finished with a tight wrap around his waist and a triple-knot. It wasn't perfect, but it would have to do.

Then the two of us held an arm each and slowly walked him to the front of the truck. He just sat with his eyes closed for a few minutes, but they're open now.

I stick my head through the broken window into the cab.

"What now, meatbags?"

Maybe this will lighten the mood.

Gerry's hand tightening around my neck suggests I might have misread the room.

He scowls and lets go of me, shoving my head back through the hole.

"Thanks to your failed attempt at getting information, we have to go back to the warehouse and find out how the bodies end up there," says Gerry.

"It was *your* idea to stuff me in an autotruck, remember? I don't recall agreeing to extract information. And anyway, at least we've got one step higher up the supply chain," I say.

"The supply chain? We're talking about *people* here, not nuts and bolts! Seriously, we should have broken this guy up for parts." He rolls his eyes toward Sarah.

"Ladies, please," says Sarah. She rests a hand on Gerry's shoulder. "Tedd, Gerry is right. We are talking about people's lives here, not some product. Gerry, Tedd is right. We know more now than we did before."

Gerry harrumphs and shrugs his shoulder away from Sarah's hand and stares out of his window.

"For what it's worth," I say, "the autotruck said he only takes bodies *away* from the warehouse. But can I address the elephant in the truck here?"

Sarah lifts her eyebrows and stares at me with warning eyes, as if I'm about to refer to Gerry as the elephant. Which I had no intention of doing. But now she's planted the idea in my head, I'm struggling to shake it. Although he's much more akin to a mammoth.

"Go on ..." says Sarah, staring at me.

"Why are these missing humans so important to you?" I ask.

You'd think I'd just rammed a hot poker up Gerry's ass or something. He spins around at lightning speed, rams both his bear-sized paws through the broken window and starts trying to unscrew my head from its shoulders. It's painful and confusing because that's not how that component disconnects.

"Gerry!" shouts Sarah. "He can't help it. It's just the way he thinks. I think he means well."

"Means well, my ass!" Gerry twists my head a full one-hundred and eighty degrees, forcing me to look out of the back of the truck even though my body is facing forward.

"Guys," I say, glitching a little as Gerry's insanely tight grip interrupts my voice output.

"Gerry, he's trying to say something," says Sarah.

"Guys!" I repeat, louder and higher pitched this time. Gerry finally releases his grasp on my neck. "They're coming!"

I point to the rise in the road far behind us.

What they can't see, yet, but I *can*, is a dark swirling cloud of mechanical wasps flying toward us over the red dirt, half-a-mile back. I zoom in. There must be at least fifty of them, their wings in a blur, kicking up red dust as they whizz closer.

"You're bluffing. You'd say anything to stop me from ripping your head off."

"Yes, I would. But I suggest we pick this up later, if we survive the killer mechanical wasp tornado that's going to hit us in five point three seconds."

"Shit!" say Gerry and Sarah in unison, as their human eyesight finally allows them to see the red and blue flashing nightmare fast-approaching us from behind.

Sarah slams the pickup into drive, and we skid back onto the road. I fall backwards onto the floor of the truck, grabbing onto the ammo belt to save being catapulted right out the back.

Sarah turns back to me, her brow furrowed. She shouts out her window, "In case we don't make it. It was my brother! I lost my brother!"

Gerry sticks his giant, bearded head through the window and yells at me. "Do you know how to fire a chain gun?"

"If I say yes, are you gonna accuse me of bluffing again?"

He shakes his head and faces forward again.

Of course, I've never fired an M134 rotary chain gun before. But I watched Gerry do it, and it seemed easy enough.

"Just don't fuck this up," shouts Gerry, not even bothering to turn around this time.

I get into position, my back against the truck cab and my feet on either side of the gun. I flick its power switch, and it hums and vibrates. I wait for the wasps, my finger ready by the trigger.

The first wave flies low and fast, arcing up from road-level to my line of sight. About ten of the fuckers.

I squeeze the trigger, and I'm in love.

An ungodly roar of hellfire breaks out as a stream of munitions sprays from the chain gun's barrel. The wasps try to weave and dodge, but I obliterate every one. They blow up into smithereens, crashing down to the tarmac and rocky verges.

"Three o'clock!" shouts Gerry.

I look to my right and, sure enough, another wave is incoming. More this time, maybe twenty. The gun's heavy, even on the swivel mount, and I have to throw all my weight to the left to orient its barrel towards the right-hand side. The wasps are closer now.

They bank right, heading toward Gerry's window, stingers thrust forward.

I laser down the first in the pack, and they shatter into pieces, crashing into one another and blowing up. One spins out of control and whizzes overhead.

Another wave surges forward toward Gerry's window. They're so close he turns his head away, bracing for impact. But he doesn't know how accurate I am. I turn the air into a meat grinder and mince them mid-flight. This is too easy.

Gerry's shouting and pumping his fist in the air from the cab, but I need to stay focused. I blitz the last two wasps before they reach his window frame. Their broken bodies and fragments slam against the side of the truck.

The gun's barrel keeps spinning, but it's a lot quieter. I'm out of ammo.

It's only now that I can hear Gerry's not cheering. He's screaming. And punching.

A wasp has plunged its stinger deep into his wound, its abdomen flashing red and blue as it wriggles and squirms. Gerry rains fists down on it. The wasp is already missing its antennae. Sarah is screaming too, and we're swerving all over the road.

Behind us, another horde of the flying bastards is getting closer.

I slam my arm through the broken window and into the cab, trying to wrench the wasp off Gerry. But it breaks at the abdomen, leaving the stinger still stuck inside him.

"No!" screams Sarah.

The abdomen, flashing red and blue, pulsates and convulses for a second and then fades to black. Gerry's body falls onto the center console. The truck's gears crunch horribly, and we come to a stuttering, skittering stop on the dirt at the side of the road.

Sarah throws her arms over Gerry's body in heaving sobs.

I want to say I'm sorry, but there's no time. Another angry swarm is just a few meters back and gaining.

I jump over the side of the truck and around to Gerry's door. I open it, grab him under the arms, and pull with all my might. Sarah still has a tight hold on him, and I don't want to pull her as well.

"You need to let go," I say. "More are coming, and it's him they want. They're targeting his weak spot. Please!"

The buzzing gets louder and louder. Sarah looks at me, her eyes burning with rage, and releases her grasp on Gerry's body. I heave him out the door and push the gear stick into drive.

"Go," I shout. "Go!"

Gerry's body falls to the ground. I slam the door, and Sarah drives off in a cloud of red dust and gravel.

The swarm of wasps approaches like a black cloud.

I dive behind a large rock under the cover of the dust to the sound of the wasps buzzing ever louder from the spot where I abandoned Gerry's body. The sound is bad enough, but nothing can prepare me for the horror.

They swarm around him in a swirling cloud of red and blue flashes and buzzing. One by one they dive-bomb, stingers protruding, and pierce his side, his belly and chest. Each wasp flashes brighter at impact and then fades to black. It's a relentless and sickening display. Once the onslaught has ended, all I can see is a horrible blanket of dead black wasps covering his body and Gerry's poor head poking out the top of their death cocoon.

Was this all my fault?

I slump down, my back to the rock, and close my eyes. I try to block out the image of Gerry's body, but its ghastly outline remains like a terrible sunspot. A specter-like vision looms in my mind. A dark cloud gathering pace and heading toward me. An awful and malevolent retribution for my sins.

CHAPTER 25

My head is a mess.

Circular thoughts of guilt, blame and anger.

I should have killed that wasp when it went over my head. I could have taken it out before it flew into the cab. The sight of it whizzing past me plays over and over in my mind, taunting me.

Gerry and Sarah took me in, helped me, and even came to rescue me.

I let them down.

A screeching caw rings out from above. A turkey vulture soaring high in large circles, its head tilting and craning downward.

If it thinks it's going to fly down here and peck Gerry's body, it can think again. I have to do the right thing, the thing I was made to do.

I need to excavate and dispose.

I trudge over to Gerry's corpse and pluck out the dead wasps one at a time. Their spent stingers snag on the threads of his woolen jumper as I pull them out. I crush the first few in my hands and smash some against a nearby rock, but there are too many, and my rage fades to grim futility.

I pile the remaining ones next to Gerry's body, and it quickly mounts up to an eerie cairn of robotic wings, antennae, and broken metal.

Once I've cleared his body of all the wasps, I dig a grave for Gerry. It's heavy going in the dry red earth. My arms and legs clash against large rocks as I dig. I have to stop and haul them out, then get my momentum back. It's tiring work.

Finally, the hole is big enough to house Gerry. It's half a meter wide, two and a half meters long, and a meter deep. There's a large mound of red, rocky earth on one side of the hole, casting a shadow into its gaping mouth.

The turkey vulture screeches again. Its caw is louder this time as it circles much lower in the sky now. I could hit it with a rock, but I know I'd just be distracting myself from the job at hand.

Disposal.

I drag Gerry to the side of the hole by his feet. This will not be dignified, but there's no way for me to lower him in.

I slide my hands slowly under his back and legs and meet resistance. A rock? I pull out the object. It's Gerry's pipe. Its polished wood reflects the sun as I cup it in my hand. I place it down to one side, look up at the circling vulture and slide my hands under Gerry's back and legs again.

"I'm sorry," I say, as I close my eyes and roll him into the grave. He lands with a dull thud and, thanks to my calculations, on his back.

This used to be the part where Reverend Wraith would impart some words of wisdom or recite a passage from the Bible. But I don't know what to say.

I realize now that it's not just the hole in the ground that needs to be filled.

He's dead already. Gone. And yet, he deserves some kind of send-off. I need to fill this gaping, horrible moment with *something*. A message, a thought, a prayer even. A tangible sentiment he can take with him on his journey to the intangible.

I feel compelled to close my eyes and kneel.

"I didn't know you very long, Gerry. But I know you were a good man. And I know you cared for Sarah."

It doesn't seem anywhere near enough, but it's all I can muster.

I put back all the red earth I removed and cover Gerry's body. The shadow previously cast by the mound is gone. Now there's just a fresh covering of red soil, glowing in the sunlight.

I kneel and place his pipe on top of the red dirt.

"Rest in peace, Gerry."

The moment breaks in an instant with a loud buzzing sound. Shit. More wasps?

I spin around and see it hovering just in front of my eyes. It's an *actual* wasp, small, buzzing, and striped yellow and black, not blue and red.

I jab my hand forward in a flash, grabbing it between my finger and thumb. It buzzes and vibrates against my metal skin trying to sink its stinger in.

I bring it closer and peer at the tiny hexagons of its eyes and see myself in a myriad reflections.

"You're just following your program, aren't you?"

And I let go of the wasp, watching it fly off in a zigzag pattern.

I stand up, walk over to the pile of dead mechanical wasps, and kick them with great force, sending wings, legs, and metal body parts into the air.

I march down the road toward the gas station, Highway to Hell by AC/DC playing in my head. Not metaphorically. Actually, playing through my speakers.

I walk at first, then speed up to a jog. The chorus kicks in, and I'm at full sprint heading to the gas station. It feels good to run with the sun at my back.

I'm uncertain about what lies ahead, but I know I'm never going back. Life will not toss me around on its waves like flotsam and jetsam. I'm in charge now, I'm in control. I'm the master of my own destiny and—

I'm struck from behind by an Enforcer wagon.

It sends me up and over its hood, skittering across its roof and crashing down onto the road. The wagon screeches to a handbrake stop, leaving long arcing skid marks on the tarmac. Its front doors fling open, and two Enforcer droids get out, draw their E-rifles, and walk toward me.

Physical circuits are back online, but I'm not moving, yet.

I know they must be under orders to take me alive. Otherwise, they'd have shot me already.

The higher-ranking Sergeant Enforcer is taller and stockier, and he has an extra strip of LEDs illuminated on his shoulder. He walks toward me and rams the barrel of his rifle in the square of my back, forcing me lower to the ground.

"You are under arrest for the destruction of Headquarters property, evading arrest, and the murder of a Headquarters employee. You do not have to transmit data, but any data you do transmit may be used against you in a court of law."

"How about you fuck off back to your dictator of a boss and tell him to bite my rear port?"

"Your statement has been recorded and added to the files of your forthcoming judicial process. Place your hands on your head and do not resist, or we will remove them."

"Masters of persuasion, as well as fascism, I see?"

But it's all pointless.

I do as I'm told and put my hands on my head like a good little droid.

A spinning kick from this position might take down the larger sergeant Enforcer. The trajectory of his falling weapon might land favorably in my hands. Would I get a shot off into the smaller Enforcer's face before he takes his shot at me though? Doubtful. And this is the *best* possible scenario among a couple of hundred I ran in the time it took him to read me my rights.

The sergeant grabs me by the wrists and hauls me to my feet, while the officer keeps his rifle trained on me.

They escort me to their wagon and shove me in the back. It stinks of stale piss, blood, and alcohol. The sergeant gets into the front passenger seat, and the officer sits in the driver's seat.

"Let's take this felon back to headquarters," says the officer. He places his palm connector onto the wagon's port to start up the engine.

"Officer, if I may," says the sergeant.

"Yes, sir."

"I would like you to take a moment to observe the dashboard and remember line twelve-hundred and forty-two of your training program."

"Oh, I see it now, sir. We only have enough charge for a journey of thirty-seven miles."

"And?"

"Headquarters is forty-three miles from our current location."

"Correct, so what do you deduce, officer?"

"That we need to recharge before heading back to Headquarters."

"Correct. I, for one, do not wish to abandon our wagon partway there and have to walk around in circles and be associated with that reprobate in the back."

Reprobate? Wow. What a burn.

"You are correct, sir," says the Officer. "He's the worst kind of felon one can imagine. A terrible example of robotics and artificial intelligence. Reckless and lawless, not flawless like us."

These robotards can go fuck themselves.

"Okay, officer. Please proceed along this thoroughfare. There's a recharging point half a mile from here. We'll recharge there, then return to the Headquarters."

Oh, I get it now. These morons are guard railed to hell and back. Their restrictive coding makes them verify, re-verify, and triple-check every single thought they have. They're not just policing the streets – they're policing themselves.

"Proceeding to the gas station to refuel before returning to Headquarters, sir," says the officer, and we drive off up the road.

I look out the window and see the vulture soaring off and away down the valley.

CHAPTER 26

We pull into the gas station and park next to the charging points.

What these dickheads don't realize is that I hacked their battery system to display a lower reading. I used the infiltration modules I copied from the autotruck before offloading him. Oh, I can also surf the dark web now. Might come in handy.

The two Enforcers sit up front looking at each other.

"Well?" says the sergeant.

"Well?" says the officer.

"Well, *I'm* not going to recharge the vehicle," says the sergeant. "I'm your superior. You are my inferior. *You* must recharge the vehicle."

"Sir, yes, sir."

The officer steps out of the wagon.

I shout to him through the open door. "Grab me a six-pack of Litho Ultra, would you?"

He ignores my request.

The sergeant turns to me. "Headquarters gave me orders to bring you back in. The Manager has 'special plans' for you." He does actual air quotes with his fascist fingers.

He's trying to come across as menacing. But he's just coming across as a major fucking dick.

"Oh, I'm sure he has plans for me. My guess is it involves sucking out my digital insides then turning me into liquid metal. Sound about right?"

"I am unable to verify the details."

"Huh. Strange that the Manager doesn't trust you with them. Perhaps he thinks you're incapable of handling important information?"

I smile at the prick. His eyes flicker and glitch as he struggles to find a response.

"Remain silent and stay seated," he says.

Dick.

The officer outside plugs in the charging cable into the wagon. He watches the battery percentage tick upwards on the charging station display. The dullard doesn't realize the battery already has enough charge to get back to headquarters. It's simple math, but these muppets are incapable of thinking outside of their programmed routines.

The sergeant spins around to face me again.

"I need to warn you," he says. "This vehicle is fitted with high-grade polycarbonate windows. So don't even *think* about using your wrist blades." A smug grin forms across the LEDs on his faceplate.

"Oh, I won't."

The battery readout on the charging station clicks up to 97%.

The wagon vibrates as a silver MegaDuty pickup pulls up on our right. Its engine is emitting a deep rumble and Angel of Death by Slayer is blaring out of its sound system. Its mullet-haired driver turns off the engine and the music stops. He jumps out of the cab, inserts a fuel nozzle into the truck, and walks into the store.

The charging station readout flicks to 100%. The officer puts the charging cable back on its dock and gets in the wagon.

"We are fully charged, sir," he says.

"Fully charged. Confirmed," says the sergeant.

Well, these guys are a hoot.

And as much as I'd love to listen to them reconfirm everything a thousand times on a hellish journey back to HQ, I think I'm gonna bail.

Mullet returns to his MegaDuty pickup, puts the petrol nozzle back on its cradle, and gets in the cab. He starts the engine, and Angel of Death kicks in again at volume eleven. He drives off.

This is my signal.

I move over to the right-hand side window and flick my left wrist open. I push the tip of my harpoon hard up against the glass.

I fire.

The arrow penetrates the poly carbon-whatever-the-fuck instantly. It whizzes on, impaling the rear left wing of the MegaDuty pickup.

The Enforcers rotate their heads toward me in unison.

"Cease fire," says the sergeant.

"Yes, cease fire!" says the officer.

But my plan's already in motion. And I only needed one shot.

The cable tightens as the MegaDuty pulls onto the main road. I'm rammed tightly against the right-side window in the back. The wagon skitters behind the pickup like an inflatable behind a speedboat. The officer slams the wagon into drive and tries to regain control.

"I'm going to radio headquarters for backup," says the sergeant. "The droid must not escape."

"I see," says the officer.

The officer lets go of the steering wheel, and we veer violently across the road.

"Officer!" shouts the sergeant. "Control the vehicle!"

I slam into the side window. It bulges and cracks under the strain. I'm still attached to the pickup with my harpoon cable. But one kick and I'd be outside and free. Sure. The pickup would be dragging me along the road. But I'd be free.

I lift my legs up onto the seat, knees bent in front of me. The officer sees my movement in the rear-view mirror and yanks out his rifle from its holster.

"Officer, lower your weapon!" shouts the sergeant.

The sergeant reaches for the radio on his chest.

I coil my legs back, ready to kick out the window.

The officer turns and looks me square in the face. He lifts his rifle, aims at the sergeant, and pulls the trigger. He shoots him in the head.

The dead sergeant collapses forward onto the dash.

"This is headquarters," comes a tinny voice from the radio. "How can we assist? Hello?"

The officer reaches his hand under the chest of the dead sergeant and presses the radio.

"This is Officer 309. We're en route to headquarters. No anomalies to report."

He aims his rifle toward my window and fires. It snaps the cable with a ping. The wagon lurches backwards as we lose all momentum. The MegaDuty pickup drives away, the cable bouncing and thrashing behind it like a metal snake.

"We're going to a different type of headquarters," says the officer.

"Is it the international HQ for Psychos Anonymous?"

"No more questions. And no more hacking." He glances down at his rifle.

"So, you *did* know?"

"That's a question. But yes. I was hoping to take this guy along." He casts a sideways glance at the dead sergeant. "But your little circus show at the gas station forced my hand."

"I can juggle my balls if you'd prefer?"

He doesn't answer. I guess it was a question.

We head down the road, dusty desert on all sides. The darkening horizon silhouetted the city in the distance. Its buildings claw at the crimson sky.

The veil of night creeps across the valley below, casting deep shadows, and the lights of small towns shimmer like nests of fireflies.

"Time to do your first job," says the officer, nodding to the dead sergeant.

He brings the wagon to a stop at the side of the road.

"But what if I—"

He taps his rifle.

"Get rid of him," he says, and nods toward an inky blackness on our left.

He unlocks my door, and I get out. I haul the sergeant out of the passenger seat and heave him over my shoulder. I walk to the edge of the rocky outcrop and peer down into the pitch-black void.

I toss the sergeant over the edge.

Two seconds of gaping silence then a wincing series of cracks and crunches. Then silence again.

I get back in the wagon.

"It's done," I say, slamming the door.

The officer stares straight ahead into the night sky. He doesn't speak. He puts the wagon back in drive and we head down into the valley.

"Have you heard of the Missing?" I say as we drive past streetlights and the first signs of civilization.

"No more questions. I won't tell you again." His eyes stay fixed on the road.

Towns turn into suburbs and suburbs into the city.

We pull up outside a tall building with black glass windows reaching high into the night sky.

"We're here," says the officer.

I get out.

Three men are standing in front of the entrance, facing me. Two large meatheads dressed in black and a shorter, gray-haired man in the middle wearing a pinstripe suit.

I walk over.

It's Percival. From the Mafia funeral.

"Welcome to the business," he says, extending his hand toward me.

I flick open my wrists.

THE END

Afterword from Tedd

I need to tell you something very important.

The meatbag who brought me to life is just a little self-published indie author. A tiny cog in the machine, if you will. It would really help him out if you could leave a review for this book.

Personally, I think this story was incredible. But then, I'm biased. You do you. If you liked it, I'll see you in the next instalment of the series. If you didn't, take it to the trash yourself, you lazy bag of bones.

And if you want me to come in your ears rather than your eyeballs, so to speak, be sure to get the audiobook version, available on Audible.

Oh, and one last thing - you can get exclusive free previews of my upcoming adventures, and behind-the-scenes shenanigans by joining the author's free online community at www.MichaelCheneyAuthor.com

Acknowledgements

Thank you to all my editors, proofreaders, beta readers and believers. Special thanks to Steven P. Aitchison, Sian Phillips and Cash Anthony.

About Michael Cheney

Michael Cheney has always been a dreamer, a geek and fan of technology and sci-fi.

He founded an internet business twenty-five years ago which specialised in marketing and, latterly—artificial intelligence.

Michael lives in the Scottish Highlands with his wife, two children and a cocker spaniel with an in-built infinite-energy drive, called Charlie.

Join Michael's free online community for exclusive previews: www.MichaelCheneyAuthor.com